DODGER
FOR
PRESIDENT

To Kelly, Kyle, & Jeremy

DODGER

FOR

PRESIDENT

JORDAN SONNENBLICK

SQUARE
FISH

FEIWEL AND FRIENDS
NEW YORK

To my beloved big sister, Lissa.
Thanks for secretly being my fan all along.

SQUARE
FISH

An Imprint of Macmillan

DODGER FOR PRESIDENT. Copyright © 2009 by Jordan Sonnenblick.
All rights reserved. Distributed in Canada by H.B. Fenn and Company Ltd.
Printed in June 2010 in the United States of America by R. R. Donnelley & Sons
Company, Harrisonburg, Virginia. For information, address Square Fish,
175 Fifth Avenue, New York, N.Y. 10010.

Square Fish and the Square Fish logo are trademarks of Macmillan and are used
by Feiwel and Friends under license from Macmillan.

Library of Congress Cataloging-in-Publication Data Available

ISBN: 978-0-312-61112-5

Originally published in the United States by Feiwel and Friends
Square Fish logo designed by Filomena Tuosto
Book design by Barbara Grzeslo
First Square Fish Edition: 2010
10 9 8 7 6 5 4 3 2 1
www.squarefishbooks.com

Look, if I'm going to tell you **everything** that happened with Lizzie and me and the fifth-grade election, you have to promise **you won't tell**. And you won't laugh—even at the parts that are really, really **funny**. And you won't mention any of this to my parents or my little sister, Amy.

Not that I care what they think.

Anyway, I guess I'll have to trust you on this, right? Plus, I'm busting to tell somebody about it. **So here goes . . .**

CHAPTER ONE

The Big Surprise

"DUDE!" DODGER SHOUTED as he jumped into my arms.

"Oww!" I yelped as we tumbled together to the floor of my room. This happened pretty often, because I was a wimpy, 80-pound fifth grader and Dodger was a really strong, 125-pound chimp. With blue fur. And bright orange-and-white surfer shorts. Plus an eye patch.

Oh, and he's invisible to everyone except me and this girl named Lizzie.

It's a really long story.

But the point is, Dodger knocked me over and

landed right on top of me. It's amazing how pointy a chimpanzee's elbows are. So as I was lying there, gasping for air, Dodger started talking a mile a minute. The conversation went like this:

DODGER: Dude, you missed so much while you were in Cleveland with your dad!

ME: *Gasp* . . .

DODGER: Lizzie took me to school, just like we planned. And there was just one little problem.

ME: *Gasp* . . .

DODGER: Like, there was this science quiz. It was totally hard. There were all these, um, questions and stuff. And you had to fill in these little bubbles with letters next to them, but I really didn't see what the letters had to do with the questions. The question would be all *What type of rock is made when a volcano erupts and then the lava cools?* But the answers would be all like *A*. Or *B*. Or *C*. Or even *D*. Dude, I don't know a whole lot about rocks, but even a chimp knows there's no kind of rock called

"A Rock." 'Cause that would be just completely confusing. Somebody would ask you, "What do you call that cool rock you're holding?" And you'd go, "This? It's called 'A Rock.'" And they'd go, "Yeah, I know it's a rock. But what kind of rock is it?" Then you'd be all, "Buddy, the *name* of this rock is 'A Rock.'" And they'd be all, "Why do you have to be such a wise guy? All I did was ask the name of a rock." So you'd go, "Exactly!" And then they'd probably hit you or something.

But, you know, I did my best for you.

ME: What do you mean, you . . . *gasp* . . . did your "best" for me?

DODGER: Well, I didn't want you to get all behind in your work, right? So I just wrote your name on top of a quiz and tried really hard to fill in all the bubbles.

ME: Okay, so you took a test in my name, on a day when I wasn't even in school. I guess that was the problem.

DODGER: Uh, no, that wasn't the problem. I mean, I made this really great sentence out of all the letters. Do you want to hear it?

ME (*puts head in hands*): *Gasp* . . . sure.

DODGER: Okay, here it is: "CAB! A CAB! DAD, A CAB! A . . . A . . . BAD CAB!" See, it's like this little story about you and your dad. Get it? You, like, see this taxicab, right? So you yell to your dad, and you try to get the driver to stop. But the cab just keeps going. Genius, huh?

ME: *Groan* . . .

DODGER: I still don't get the part about the rocks, though. Well, maybe we'll get a lot of points for creativity.

You couldn't leave this chimp alone for a minute. So apparently a whole weekend plus a school day were completely out of the question. I got up off the floor, checked myself for broken ribs, and dusted off. Meanwhile Dodger started to tell me about the rest of his day at school. It was hard to believe there was more, but I hadn't even heard about the problem yet.

6

"So then in social studies, they're learning about how all these explorer guys discovered North America and discovered South America and, like, discovered Africa. I totally wanted to set the record straight, but I didn't."

Well, that was a relief. "Uh, Dodger, what did you want to set the record straight about, exactly?"

"I wanted to tell them about how chimpanzees had already totally conquered all those places, thousands and thousands of years ago. Like before you called it South America, we called it Banana World. And before you had Europe, we had No-Monkeys-Land."

I always get drawn in when he does this. I don't know why, but it happens every stupid time. So I said, "What about Asia?"

He smirked. "Chimptopia, of course."

"Africa?"

"Land O'Mammals."

"New Jersey?"

Dodger made a horrified face. "Dude, who would want to conquer New Jersey? Anyway, you would have been proud of me, Willie. I didn't say a single word. Well, okay, I kind of laughed when the cake fell on James Beeks."

"Wait a minute, a cake fell on James Beeks? Was *that* the problem?"

" 'Problem'? It was awesome. I mean, there was this huge, brown-and-orange volcano cake on the ledge over the chalkboard. And, you know, Beeks is the coolest kid in the school, right? And he always calls you Wimpy and says you're a total dork, right? So I just thought it was funny when he got . . ."

"What do you mean, a total dork?" I blurted.

Dodger looked sheepish for a moment. "Well, you know, not a dork, exactly. It's not your fault about your little dressing-funny problem, since your mom picks out all your clothes, right? Plus, who can blame you for not having any guy friends since Tim moved away? It's hard to hang out with the guys if you're not good at—oh, never mind."

I was insulted, but I forced myself to take a deep breath. The madder I got, the more off topic Dodger got, and I had a feeling I would really need to know what the mysterious problem was. "Whatever. So how did the cake fall on James Beeks anyway?"

"Okay, you know how I was trying not to say anything about the whole social studies thing? That was totally hard for me, right? So I was just kind of hopping up and down in my seat next to Lizzie. I guess that made the ledge over the chalkboard vibrate. And the cake just slid off the ledge. Then Mrs. Starsky tried to make a jumping catch. It was pretty awesome, but she fumbled the cake. So it bounced off her hands onto James's head, upside down."

I could just tell there had to be more to this story, so I waited. Sure enough, Dodger continued, "I don't know why he got so mad. I only laughed a little. And it's not like my laugh really sounds like Lizzie's anyway. But he thought Lizzie was laughing at him—I guess he couldn't hear that well through all the cake around his ears. So he got all mad, and Mrs. Starsky yelled at Lizzie."

"Oh," I said. "I guess that's the problem, huh?"

"No," Dodger replied. "That's not the problem. So then Lizzie started yelling at James, right? And, dude, he was getting completely heated. He kept trying to wipe all this orange icing off his face and yelling back at her. Then Mrs. Starsky was standing between James and Lizzie, trying to see if James was okay, even though it was only a cake that fell on him in the first place. It was really funny, but I only laughed a little bit more. So the teacher thought it was Craig Flynn, 'cause he usually laughs at everybody, right?"

This was getting better and better. *Not!* I thought I heard our doorbell ringing downstairs, but I wasn't going to go down and miss the end of this story. My mom could get the door.

"Everybody was going totally bananas. I mean, you know I love bananas, but—I mean, everyone was going nuts—well, I like nuts, too, but you know what I mean. Lizzie and James were yelling at each other; Mrs. Starsky was yelling at Craig; and Craig was just standing there totally confused and wondering who he should blame for the whole thing so he could beat them up at lunch recess. Then somehow it wound up that Craig, Mrs. Starsky, and James were all looking right at Lizzie."

Wow. "So that was the problem, huh?"

"Nope," said Dodger. Just then, I heard footsteps charging up the stairs. Dodger looked at my bedroom door and gulped. "The problem—and it's really just a teeny little problem. I mean, fifth grade isn't really a very long part of your life span, when you think about it." Dodger swallowed again and said, "The problem is—"

Lizzie burst into the room, causing the door to bang off the wall. She was out of breath, but she immediately said, "Dodger, did you tell Willie about the class election?"

I looked at Dodger. Lizzie saw my confused face, then glared at Dodger. I said, "Election?"

Dodger looked like he was going to throw up. "Dude," he said, "*that's* the problem!"

CHAPTER TWO

Who Knew Chimps Were So into Politics?

I TURNED TO LIZZIE and asked, "What's Dodger talking about?"

She was all flustered, and I noticed she didn't look me in the eye. "Hi, Willie!" she said brightly as she came over and gave me a hug.

Jeepers. Lizzie was giving me a hug!

As she let go of me, Lizzie kept talking a mile a minute. "How are you? Did you have fun traveling with your dad? Did you have smooth flights? I really hate when I'm on a bumpy flight. I remember this one time, on the way back to England to visit my aunt Mimi, we hit this massive turbulence over the Atlantic. It was just *dreadful*! My teacup flew up in the air and flipped over. I got tea all over this horrid bald man who was sitting next to me, and he said—"

"LIZZIE!" I shouted.

"No, he didn't say 'Lizzie,' actually. In fact, I'm not sure I ever told him my—"

"Lizzie! Stop trying to distract me! What's this whole election thing about?"

Lizzie practically turned green, so I knew that, whatever was going on, hearing about it wasn't going to send me to my happy place. As she gathered herself to speak, I noticed that Dodger was trying to crawl under my bed to hide. I guess he hadn't ever noticed how much stuff I shove down there so my mom will think my room is clean.

Lizzie said, "The election? Right, then. The election. Hmm . . . well, the thing is, there's this election. You know, for the student council president? And James Beeks is running for president, with Craig Flynn as his vice president. See, every year at our school, the fifth graders elect a president and a vice president for the grade, and those officers are also the president and vice president of the student council. Really, it's quite a fascinating blend of British and American political—"

"*Ahem.*" I cleared my throat and tried to ignore the dirt-encrusted sweat sock that Dodger's hand was pushing out from under the bed. "Lizzie, I know all about how our school's elections work, so stop stalling. I want to know what this has to do with us."

Lizzie's voice was a squeak. "With *us?*" she asked. "Well, I've always thought that everyone should get involved in the process of government. Don't you agree?"

I glared at Lizzie as Dodger shoved another disgusting sock into view behind her. " 'Involved'? What do you mean, *involved?*"

A half-eaten slice of pizza, covered in dust bunnies and clumps of hair, slid out from Dodger's hiding place. Then it slid back in, and in the silence while Lizzie tried to figure out what to tell me, I could distinctly hear munching noises. *Eww!* I was just about to gag when Lizzie finally spoke. If I'd thought she was talking fast before, this took the speed to a whole new level.

"Well, Dodger and I had a little, umm, incident

with James Beeks and Craig Flynn. You know, because Dodger was you today, and all."

"What do you mean, Dodger was me?"

I heard a little choking sound coming from under the bed, and Dodger's hands appeared. Now Lizzie looked more puzzled than afraid. "You know," she said. "With the potion. Just like you planned."

Dodger pulled himself out from under the bed and sat up, coughing and grabbing at his throat the whole time. "Potion?" I asked. What was Lizzie talking about? Now I was more confused than ever. "Dodger, what in the world is going on?"

Dodger suddenly made a little burping noise, and something flew into his hands. "Nothing, dude. Just a little pepperoni hair ball."

Aargh!

Lizzie said, "Dodger told me everything this morning on the way to the bus stop: how the Great Lasorda gave him this special potion that would let him look like you for the day, and that way he could start Phase Two of your Life Improvement Plan."

"Life Improvement Plan?"

"Right, just like Dodger said. He came to school

disguised as you and started looking for ways to make you popular. The Great Lasorda said that because Dodger is so naturally fun to be around, he should have no problem making your social life more, um, interesting."

That's weird, because in the past month, my only friend had moved away, a magical chimp had pledged to be my new best friend for life, and I had somehow become good pals with the girl I used to call "dumb old Lizzie from England." Wasn't my social life interesting enough?

I stared at Lizzie, speechless. I mean, I had plenty to say, but I was having trouble deciding which of my crazy friends to shout at first. Behind her, Dodger wiped his hands on one of the socks, which he proceeded to shove back under my bed. And then my little sister, Amy, came stalking into the room, wearing a bizarre hat with flaps and my dad's checkered raincoat. She was carrying a magnifying glass. "A-ha!" she shouted in a boomingly dramatic voice. "Just as I suspected, Watson!"

Lizzie said, "Hello, Amy. How are you today?"

Amy replied disdainfully, "I am not Amy. If you had any powers of deduction whatsoever, you would infer from my clothing that I am Sherlock Holmes, the greatest detective of all time. And I know you are keeping a secret!"

Jeepers, this was just getting better and better. As if having an invisible houseguest wasn't hard enough already, now I had a deluded second grader sniffing around the joint, looking for signs of mystery and intrigue.

"What secret?" I asked in my best innocent voice. "Lizzie and I were just having a friendly chat."

Amy hunched over her magnifying glass and scuttled around the room like a crab, examining the floor as she went. Dodger nearly tripped over himself twice as he tried to stay ahead of her. She was talking to herself under her breath, saying detective-ish things like, "Hmm . . . uh-huh . . . interesting . . . very interesting . . ." Then all of a sudden, she stood bolt upright and shouted, "Eureka! I knew it!"

Lizzie and I both said, "Knew what?"

Amy scooped up the filthy sock, waved it under our noses, and exclaimed, "Knew I'd find this!"

I was baffled, and somewhat irritated. "Wow,

Amy, you found one of my socks. In my room. You're a genius! But what does it mean?"

"The name is Sherlock. And the sock is a very important clue. Note the grimy exterior, which indicates that the sock has been worn repeatedly without washing. Take notice, too, of the powerful scent emitted by this discarded garment. Finally, observe this!" She pinched something on the sock and held it up to the light. "A blue hair!"

Oh, boy. I had a sinking feeling that Amy wasn't going to let go of this one. She paused for a moment and then said in her normal voice, "By the way, Willie, can you help me with my math homework?"

"Uh, I'm kind of busy right now, but I guess if you make it quick . . ."

"All right, then. I'm a little confused. What does one plus one make?"

I wondered how a kid with such an amazing imagination could be so bad at math. "Uh, Amy, one plus one equals two."

"I see . . . and there's one of you in this room, plus one of Lizzie, right?" Amy said. Then she suddenly switched back to her Sherlock voice and

18

asked, "Then why did I hear THREE voices in this room before I came in?"

With a triumphant smirk, Amy flipped the sock in my direction and glided out of the room. I slammed the door behind her.

"Wow." Lizzie sighed.

"Yeah," I said, removing the sock from the front of my sweater. "Wow. Now, about that election."

"We didn't mean it, Willie. It just kind of happened," Dodger said. "One minute, everything was going great. I drank the potion, pretended to be you for a couple of hours, took that quiz I was telling you about, watched the cake fall on James Beeks—it was all fun and games. Then all of a sudden, everybody was yelling at each other, and I had to stick up for Lizzie. The next thing I knew . . . umm . . . well . . ."

Lizzie took over: "The next thing he knew, Mrs. Starsky was walking out of the room to the water fountain so she could wash the cake off of her shoes. As soon as she left, Beeks said, 'Shut up, Wimpy. You think you're so great now just because you got one lucky game-tying hit in one stupid baseball game. Well, I think you're ridiculous. You got one hit. ONE hit. And all of a sudden, a few people pat you on the back, you have your dorky English girlfriend, and you think you're popular. Is that it, Ryan? Do you think you're all popular now?' "

Dodger took over the story: "I tried not to say anything, I really did. But, dude, he called Lizzie dorky. And he insulted your big hit. So I just said, 'Maybe.' Then Beeks poked me in the chest, and said, 'Maybe WHAT, Wimpy?' So I said, 'Maybe I'm popular. And maybe you should wipe the cake off your head before you call somebody else ridiculous.' After that, things got a little out of hand."

I shouted, "After THAT, things got out of hand? How much more out of hand could they possibly BE?"

Dodger and Lizzie hemmed and hawed for a while more, and little Sherlock Holmes knocked on the door two more times, but I eventually got the whole story: how Mrs. Starsky had come back from the hall with her shoes dripping and separated Dodger and Beeks. How they had kept yelling at each other until Mrs. Starsky had written both my name and Beeks's on the board. How Beeks had challenged Dodger to run against him for student council president. How Flynn had muttered, "Yeah, right. Wimpy for president!" How Dodger had stopped for a second to think. And how, in the momentary silence, Lizzie had slammed her palms down on her desk and shouted, "We accept!"

After Lizzie left, and Dodger fled to the inside of his magic lamp for the night, I got ready for bed. While I was lying there in the dark, I kept picturing the whole nightmare classroom scene in my head and wondering what the heck I was going to do about it. Finally, before I drifted off into a night of nervous, tortured half-sleep, I decided what I would have to do. I'd just get up in the morning, march off to school, and tell Mrs. Starsky that I was sorry, but I couldn't run for president after all. I mean, Dodger had gotten all worked up in the spirit of the moment and put me in a bad situation. But I had spent years carefully avoiding the spotlight. If I backed down, Beeks would probably make fun of me for a while, but soon things would be back to normal. I would be happily invisible, Beeks would get elected, just like he had every year since kindergarten, and life would go on.

I figured, how hard could it be? It's not like one day of being absent could change my life forever, right?

CHAPTER THREE

Making My Own Decisions

THE NEXT MORNING, bright and early, I ran up to my classroom before school started. Mrs. Starsky was just getting there, wearing a brand-new pair of icing-free shoes. "Hello, Willie!" she said. "How's our school's newest political candidate doing today?"

I looked down at the floor—which still had a vivid orange volcano-cake stain—and said, "Uhh, about that candidate thing . . . I've thought it over, and I don't think I want to run for president after all. I didn't really want to run in the first place."

Mrs. Starsky looked sort of puzzled. "But, Willie," she said, "you seemed so fired up about it just a day ago. What happened?"

"I don't know," I mumbled. "I guess I just wasn't myself yesterday. And running wasn't even my idea."

Mrs. Starsky gave me the dreaded Understanding Teacher Smile. "Oh, William. I have a little story I think you should hear. Why don't you have a seat?"

I sat, and she launched into one of those inspiring pep-talk stories that teachers save up for these special moments. "You're not going to believe this, Willie, but I was once a shy kid."

Mrs. Starsky had been *shy*? I found that hard to believe—this was a woman who sang "The Star-Spangled Banner" on the intercom every day during morning announcements. Even though she was 100 percent tone-deaf.

"But then my best friend persuaded me to try out for the middle-school cheerleading squad. She was always much more daring than I was—kind of like your fearless friend, Lizzie. I tried my hardest to get out of trying out. I pretended my throat

hurt. I tried to tell the coach I had a sprained ankle. I even claimed that someone else had signed
my name on the tryout list—can you believe that?"

I smiled at her. Weakly.

"But my friend wouldn't give up on me, and
when the day came, there I was, standing on the
line at the edge of the basketball court in a hot-
pink leotard."

Eww.

Mrs. Starsky beamed at me. "By the end of the
session, I even found the courage to let myself get
flung up in the air from the top of a pyramid for-
mation. So you see, Willie, sometimes you have to
rise to a new challenge, even if you do have some
second thoughts the morning after." Shaking my
head to erase the weird image of Mrs. Starsky flying through the air waving pom-poms, I asked,
"So, what happened with the tryout? Did you
make the team?"

Just then, the bell rang to let everyone into the
building. "Ooh, look at the time! This was a lovely
chat, Willie, but I have to write the homework on
the chalkboard now. Please think about what I've
said, all right? If you still really want to drop out

of the election, you can let me know by three PM today."

"Oh, come on, Mrs. Starsky. You can't tell me ninety percent of the story and then not let me know how it ended. Please tell me what happened."

She laughed nervously.

"Please? Just tell me—did you make the team?"

"Well," she said, "I didn't quite . . . I mean . . . there was a little problem with the pyramid stunt. But the dentists at the hospital did a great job of fixing my front teeth. And in the end—after some minor plastic surgery—I learned some important life lessons."

Swell, I thought. She tried the new experience and escaped with nothing worse than a smashed-up face. That was tremendously comforting. As the rest of the class arrived, I thought about Mrs. Starsky's request to wait until the end of the day to drop out of the race. I didn't see the point because the facts weren't going to change by then. Math was math. In the margin of my notebook, I started to write down the equations that would control the outcome of the election:

Me = Dork
Lizzie = Dork
James = Popular Kid
Craig Flynn = Scary Tough Kid
Popular Kid + Scary Tough Kid = Unbeatable Combo
Dork + Dork = <u>Very</u> Beatable Combo with Possibility of
    Record-Breaking Landslide Defeat

My pencil point broke, and I got up to sharpen it. When I got back, Dodger was standing silently next to my seat. I waved him away, and he strolled over to take a nap in his favorite spot on top of the radiator. Sitting back down, I saw that Dodger had added another line to my calculations:

Dork + Dork + Magic = FUN!!!

I groaned. As you can probably tell, Dodger's definition of *fun* was remarkably similar to my definition of *trouble*.

At lunch, I told Lizzie about my conversation with Mrs. Starsky. She spent the next twenty minutes attempting to convince me that I should run no matter what happened. Then we went outside for recess, sat down under a tree, and kept right on arguing.

Two shadows fell over us. I looked up into the sneering faces of James and Craig. "So," James said, "are you planning your election campaign or your wedding?"

"Ooh, good one," Lizzie retorted. "Did you think of that by yourself, or did you ask a first grader for help?"

James said, "You know you're totally going to lose, don't you? I mean, I'm the best candidate. I've been on student council since kindergarten, and I have tons of friends. And you're—well—you're *you*."

Lizzie stayed calm. Looking James right in the eye, she said, "You know, the election isn't just a popularity contest. A lot of kids in our grade would be happy to vote for an intelligent, thoughtful candidate who has a good understanding of the issues surrounding—HEY, WHAT ARE YOU LAUGHING AT?"

James was practically doubled over with glee. "The issues," he wheezed between fits of laughter. "She thinks the election is about the issues. Ooh, that's a good one. The *issues!*"

"Okay, Mr. Expert, what is the election about, then?"

"It's about me being the best, and everybody else knowing it. And if you know what's good for you, you'll get your *friend* here to drop out of the race before things get really embarrassing."

Lizzie was fuming. When I was little, there was this kid named Davey on our block. Davey had this tiny, short-legged lapdog that looked like the weakest animal in the world. The first time I met Davey, I asked him the name of the dog, and he said, "Bloodfang." I almost laughed. But then, about a week later, I saw a huge German shepherd running past my house in a panic. A moment later, Bloodfang came charging after it. That German shepherd practically ran up a tree to escape Bloodfang's rage, and I don't think it ever came back to our street.

If James didn't back off fast, he was going to find out that Lizzie's parents should have named her Bloodfang.

"Listen, James," I said. "I don't really want to run anyway. So I'm sure we could work this out so that everybody is happy if you'll just stop being so insulting."

Lizzie elbowed me aside. "Yeah, James. We'll drop out of the race. All you have to do is ask nicely."

Craig, who hadn't said a word this whole time, said to James, "Hey, that sounds fair. Why don't you just ask the dorks—sorry, Willie . . . sorry, Lizzie—to drop out?"

James whirled to glare at his running mate. "James Beeks doesn't ASK, Craig. James Beeks TELLS. James Beeks has been running unopposed in these elections for years, and he isn't about to stop now." He turned back to stare down at us. "What do you say to that, Lizzie?"

"I say James Beeks sounds like a moron when he talks about himself in the third person."

"Okay, how about you, Wimpy? Are you ready to step aside and let a real man run, or are you and your ugly girlfriend going to embarrass your-selves even more than usual?"

Lizzie bit her lip. She didn't look very Bloodfang-ish anymore. In fact, she looked like she might be about to cry. Suddenly, I heard an angry voice. Alarmingly, the voice was coming from my mouth: "Oh, we're running, Beeks. And we're going to kick your sorry butts!"

Oh, man, I thought. *I've definitely been hanging out with Lizzie and Dodger too much.*

At the end of the day, I told Mrs. Starsky I would stay in the election. She smiled radiantly at me and said, "Excellent! I've been itching for a real election campaign around here for years. We'll set the elections for two weeks from now, right before Thanksgiving. This will be a great learning experience for all of us!"

As the afternoon sunlight slanting through the classroom windows reflected off her teeth, I was pretty sure I could see a line where one had broken off and been glued back together. I gulped, and prayed that my learning experience with the election would work out better than hers had with the pyramid.

On my way out of the building, I passed the

gym, where a bunch of James Beeks's cool female friends were already practicing cheers for him:

"Yeah, James! Go, Beeks!
We know you can beat the geeks!"

It was going to be a long two weeks.

CHAPTER FOUR

Three Exclamation Points

"SO," DODGER SAID, standing on his hands and leaning his feet against the wall, "what's our strategy, dude?"

We were in the family room at my house after school. My mom had set us up with a snack of apples, then gone outside to work in the yard. Lizzie and I were munching on the apples. Dodger had just gobbled down an entire bunch of bananas that he had pulled out of his Bottomless Well of Treats, a magical bag that filled up with whatever food you wished for. I had had a little mishap with the bag right after I'd met Dodger, so now it had a big patch on the bottom. Also, everything that came out of it tasted a little bit like milk and chocolate doughnuts.

Long story.

Anyhow, we were having the first meeting of what Lizzie insisted on calling, "Team Ryan-Barrett!!!" I had asked her jokingly whether the three exclamation points were optional, and she had replied with an icy no. As if the only thing standing between us and total victory was a lack of exciting punctuation.

Lizzie called the meeting to order—no, I'm not kidding—and took out a yellow legal pad and a pencil. "Good question, Dodger," she said. "What *is* our strategy?"

Dodger did a back handspring, landed on the big comfy chair, burped, and said, "Beats me. Willie's the one running for president. He must have some truly excellent ideas. Right, Willie?"

I just looked at him blankly.

After an uncomfortably long silence, Lizzie said, "All right, we'll get back to strategy later, if

34

there's time. Meanwhile, how about we list our strengths?"

I snorted. "Now *that* shouldn't take long," I said. "Can I see that pencil for a minute?" She handed it over, and I made a little chart on the pad:

STRENGTHS

Beeks-Flynn	Ryan-Barrett
Popularity	Abundant banana supply
Government experience	Abundant banana supply
Vice pres. candidate is intimidating	Vice pres. is great with punctuation
Cheerleaders	Chimp

Lizzie yanked the paper away from me, and her eyebrows wrinkled up as she read it. "Willie, why in the world are you running if you think we're doomed from the start?"

"Beesh call boo uggy," I muttered into my armpit.

"What did you say?" Lizzie asked.

I felt really funny about saying it more clearly,

35

but Dodger apparently didn't have the same problem. He blurted out, "Willie said, Beeks called you ugly."

Then a horrifying thing happened. Lizzie got all misty-eyed, stood up from her chair, and patted me on the arm. "You're defending my honor! Oh, Willie!"

"Oh, Willie!" Dodger giggled.

Just then, Amy tromped into the room in her Sherlock gear. " 'Oh, Willie,' what?"

Lizzie gave me one more dreamy look, sat back down, and filled in little Sherlock on our whole campaign situation. At the end, she asked, "So, what do you think? You're a great detective—how should we proceed with this case?"

"This isn't a case," Amy said. "It isn't even much of a mystery." She paused dramatically to look through her magnifying glass at a bit of banana peel that had fallen onto the table. Lizzie, Dodger, and I all leaned closer to hear her next words.

"Your only chance," Amy continued, "is to

fight dirty." Then she raised an eyebrow, took a tweezers and a plastic bag out of her coat pocket, and confiscated the shred of banana peel as evidence.

Amy walked out, and I said, "What does she mean, our only chance is to fight dirty? We're honest. We're noble. We're the good guys."

Amy popped her head back in the doorway. "You're the *dead* guys."

I threw a sofa pillow at her, and she disappeared from sight. This time I waited until I heard her bedroom door slamming upstairs before I said anything else. "Is she right? Is cheating our only chance?"

Dodger looked disgusted. He said, "Dude, I hate cheating. The Great Lasorda was always trying to get me to cheat for my clients. I think we should win this thing the old-fashioned way."

"With intelligence?" Lizzie asked.

"No," Dodger said.

"With a carefully balanced platform that meets voters' needs?"

"No."

37

"With family values and good old American know-how?"

"Nope." He stopped to pick some mushed banana out of his chest hair and then licked his fingers with satisfaction. "With free food!"

You know what? It takes a whole heck of a lot of wishing and stacking to get a whole school's worth of doughnuts from a Bottomless Well of Treats. Plus, let me tell you, smuggling four hundred doughnuts out of the house when you live with a suspicious detective is no bargain either. Dodger and I had to get up at five AM. Then I had to sneak down into the garage, climb out the window, and stand in the middle of a pricker bush while Dodger tossed down several garbage bags full of doughnuts. Next I had to hide the bags behind the bush, climb back into the garage, sneak to my room, and try to go back to sleep with Dodger bouncing around, going, "Hey, since we're up, let's play! Do you have any cards? I love War. Man, I RULE at that game. Once, when I was stuck in my lamp under a lily pad in the middle of a pond for twelve years with nothing to entertain me but a pack of cards, I figured out an unbeatable system for winning at War. There was this school of guppies that always wanted to play Go Fish, but I was like, 'Why does it always have to be about you?'"

By the time he finally stopped to take a breath, I was nearly asleep again, but I managed to groan, "Dodger, you do realize that War is totally a game of luck."

He didn't say anything for a while, so I said, "Uh, you do know that, don't you?"

He was still silent. "Dodger?"

Then he punched me on the arm and doubled over with laughter. "Oh, dude, you really had me going there for a minute. War is a game of *luck*? That's a riot!"

I rubbed my arm, rolled over, sat up, and looked at Dodger. This was great. My magical, invisible campaign strategist thought War was a game of skill.

When I finally gave up on sleep, got up, and stumbled out to go to the bathroom, the last thing I heard was Dodger muttering, "Wow . . . next he'll be trying to tell me that the dinosaurs were real!"

Dodger and I walked to school really early with our garbage bags full of doughnuts (because it wouldn't be good if someone was looking and saw several black bags floating through the air) and met Lizzie, who had brought paper plates and napkins. Dodger loped off into the fields behind the school. As he was leaving, I asked him what he was going to do all day, and he winked at me with his unpatched eye. "Meet me in our spot after school," he said.

Jeepers. I hoped he wasn't up to something.

Lizzie and I set up a folding table that Lizzie had arranged to borrow from the custodians, and when the school buses pulled up, our campaign began. I'm pretty sure we gave at least one doughnut to every kid in the school except James and Craig, and even Craig grabbed a doughnut from the hands of a frightened third grader. Craig was standing about fifty feet away from us with James, who was handing out hundreds of buttons. Craig kept sneaking bites of the doughnut, and then Beeks would catch him and smack his arm. I couldn't tell what the buttons said, but I wasn't looking forward to finding out. All of Beeks's cool-kid friends laughed their heads off as they pinned the buttons on themselves. Some other kids took them and laughed, while a smaller group took them and looked disgusted.

One little second grader took a button, read it, and then kicked Beeks in the shin. I'd never been prouder of my little detective.

Finally, a kid in our class named Joey Carbone, who had a broken leg, hobbled over to us on his crutches to get a doughnut. In order to grab one, he had to drop his things on the table in front of Lizzie. One of the buttons was attached to his backpack strap; it read:

BEEKS > FREAKS

Joey looked horrified when he realized Lizzie had read the button, but she just smiled and said,

"Joseph, I suppose you will have to decide which is more important to you in a candidate: cruelty or sweetness." Then she held a doughnut just out of his reach. He took the button off of his backpack and threw it in the garbage next to the table. "A wise choice," Lizzie said, and handed Joey his doughnut.

Right before the late bell rang, Lizzie and I treated ourselves to two of the last three doughnuts. While we were eating, one of Beeks's cheerleaders came up to us and said, "Hey, Willie, you have a little chocolate smeared under your nose." I tried to wipe it off while she played around with her cell phone—which you're not even supposed to have at school in the first place, but whatever. She kept pushing buttons on the phone as she said, "Higher, Willie. Almost got it . . . a little to the left . . ." Then I heard a click, just as she exclaimed, "Perfect!" and skipped off to class.

I had no idea what that had been about. The popular girls were even stranger than Lizzie!

We folded up our table, cleaned up our stuff,

and rushed off to class. I gave Mrs. Starsky the last doughnut, and she told me, "You know I don't get to vote, right?" Then she winked at me. What was this, Wink at Willie Day?

CHAPTER FIVE

Playing Fair

AS SOON AS SCHOOL LET OUT, Lizzie and I took off for the woods. Dodger had said to meet him in our spot, which means the secret clearing in the forest that only Lizzie and I could see. It's called the Field of Dreams, and Dodger could magically transform it into any kind of place he wanted—well, except that nearly everything in the field was always blue. When we got there, we found Dodger sitting on a blue beanbag chair, under a blue tree, watching a blue TV with a built-in digital video player, which was plugged into a blue battery.

He was smiling. And eating, as usual.

"Hi, Dodger," I said. "What have you been doing all day?"

"Research, dude. Want some blueberry pie?"

"No, thank you."

"Lizzie, some blue-corn tortilla chips with blue cheese dressing?"

"No, thanks."

I couldn't contain my curiosity. I blurted out, "What research?"

"Well, we needed some, like, scientific information about elections. So I watched some totally useful movies about government. And let me tell you, I learned a *lot*."

"Such as?" Lizzie asked.

"Let's see." He rummaged through a stack of DVDs he had piled up on the ground. "Ooh, here's an excellent resource."

"*Bugs Bunny in King Arthur's Court*?"

"Yeah, buddy! From this fine film, I learned that you definitely shouldn't cheat if you want to win. King Arthur believed in being fair to everybody, and he got elected."

"But . . . but . . . ," I stammered, "King Arthur

wasn't a president. He never even got elected. He was a king!"

Dodger shrugged. "Huh, how 'bout that?" he said. "But, dude, that's only one example." He waved another video case at me. "Like, in this movie, there's this little mermaid, and she almost loses her swimming-princess job forever, but then she's nice and sings really cool songs and stuff. And this dancing crab helps her get elected to be a princess again."

"She doesn't get elected. She just marries a prince. Princesses don't get elected either. It's, um, automatic."

"Oh. Well, I still learned stuff. Here's an example: If some evil person acts like she's suddenly trying to help you, you prob'ly shouldn't let her."

"I'll keep that in mind." Yeah, right. In case a sea witch came around and tried to trick me.

Lizzie grabbed the next case on the pile. "Hey, Dodger, did you watch *The Polar Express* today?"

"Uh, yeah."

"What does that have to do with elections?"

"Nothing. But I thought I deserved a break after doing all that heavy research."

Lizzie shook her head to clear it, as if there were water in her ears. Dodger sometimes had that effect on my brain, too.

"So," I said, "what's the next phase of our election plan?"

Lizzie said, "It's time to examine our electoral demographics."

"Our electro-whoosie ma-whatsits?"

Lizzie rolled her eyes. "Electoral demographics. Honestly, Willie, don't you ever look at *The New York Times*?"

"Uh, not so much, no. Is that, like, some special clock?"

She sighed. "No, Willie, it's not some special clock—it's the most important newspaper in the world. And electoral demographics means taking a look at which groups of people are probably going to vote for us, which groups of people *might* vote for us, and which groups of people probably aren't going to vote for us. Then we can figure out how to get our message out to the voters we need the most."

"Uh, okay," I said. "Hey, Lizzie, why don't you make a nice chart of the projectoral memographics, and Dodger and I can take a little nap break?"

Dodger gave me a high five and immediately put his feet up on the blue tree. Then he whipped out an extra eye patch, put it on his unpatched eye, sank back into his beanbag chair, and started to snore dramatically.

Lizzie said, "I can't do this alone, Willie. The election will be upon us before you know it, and we have to come up with an overall strategy. Here! Take this marker and set up a chart."

She bossed me around for a while, as Dodger made some extremely powerful snoring noises. We argued back and forth for a while. My first chart looked like this:

Will Vote for Us	Might Vote for Us	Would Only Vote for Us if We Held Their Moms Hostage or Offered Them a Million Dollars (or both)
Willie Ryan	Joey Carbone	Beeks & Flynn
Lizzie Barrett	Chess Team	Anyone popular
	That one kid who got kicked off the chess team for being too dorky	Anyone athletic
		Anyone who's afraid of Flynn
		Anyone who wants to be popular or athletic

"All right," Lizzie said. "That's a good start."

"How is that a good start?" I asked. "It looks like we're going to get killed!"

"Ah, but it also tells us what we have to do if we *don't want* to get killed."

"Huh?"

"Willie, all we have to do is position you as athletic, popular, and somewhat fearsome, while retaining your core qualities of honesty and goodness."

"Oh, is that all? While we're at it, why don't we convince the whole school that I'm a world-class surfing champion? Or a legendary movie stuntman? Or that there's a whole series of best-selling books about me and my invisible friend?"

"Very funny, Willie. Now, can we get down to business? First, how are we going to make you seem athletic?"

Dodger pulled his spare eye patch up onto his forehead. Apparently he hadn't actually been sleeping. "Lizzie, what do you mean, make him *seem* athletic? You're talking about Willie Ryan, the kid who hit the game-tying double in the fall Little League championships. Remember?"

"Yes, I do. But nobody else will. And even if they do, Beeks will say, 'So what, it was just one little hit. And *I'm* James Beeks.'"

"Okay," I said, "maybe we should get back to the athletic part later. How about the popular part?"

Lizzie just stared at me.

"Well, what about the fearsome part?"

Lizzie smiled grimly and cracked her knuckles. "Don't worry, you can leave the fearsome part to me."

I believed her. "And the honesty and goodness?"

Dodger said, "Dude. Just be yourself!"

Just then, Lizzie snapped her fingers. "I've got it!" she exclaimed. "Posters!"

Wow, posters. What a brilliant new idea.

She looked at Dodger. "Dodger, do you have a camera?"

Without even sitting up, Dodger reached into the huge pocket of his baggy orange shorts and pulled out the Bottomless Well of Treats. Then he stuck his arm into the bag, groped around for a while, and yanked out a blue camera. He tossed the camera backward over his shoulder.

Lizzie scrambled to catch it, but made a disgusted face when she did. "Ugh," she said, wiping chocolate, powdered sugar, and what appeared to be a blue hairball off her hands onto the leg of her jeans.

"What?" Dodger asked.

She sighed. "Nothing."

I sidled over to Lizzie and checked out the camera. It was awesome! I don't know much about photography, but I could tell this thing was fancy. It had a huge zoom lens, a million buttons, and a big display window on the back. On the side, in large block letters, it said OCHYMPUS.

"So we have a camera—now what?" I asked.

Lizzie grabbed Dodger by the elbow and started whispering in his ear. He whispered something back, and then they put their heads together and totally ignored me while they figured out a whole photo campaign. I walked around the meadow, kicking a little blue rock and trying not to think of all the embarrassing things Dodger and Lizzie would probably make me do.

When they called me back over, I couldn't believe it. They actually had some excellent ideas. For the first time, I started to believe I might even get more than two votes in the election.

Lizzie grabbed the camera and Dodger pulled me behind a tree.

"What are you doing?" I hissed.

Dodger gave me his biggest, goofiest grin, and said, "Costume time!"

He waved his hand at me, and suddenly I was wearing a beautiful baseball uniform. I stepped out from behind the tree, and Lizzie started clicking away. Then she pushed me behind the tree, and Dodger changed my wardrobe again. By the fourth set of pictures, I was seeing flashes of color everywhere I looked, and my cheeks hurt from smiling on cue. This candidate stuff was hard work.

But soon we were done. Dodger and Lizzie sent me home and told me they had to go to the local copy shop to get the photos made into posters. "Wait," I said. "Why don't you just make the posters magically?"

Dodger looked hurt. "What do you think I am?" he asked. "A miracle worker?"

Two hours later, I was doing homework in my room when my mom came to tell me that Lizzie was at the door. "You sure are seeing a lot of that girl lately," she said with a smirk. "Oh, my little boy is growing up so fast! But, Willie, try to comb your hair before she sees you, okay?" Just a few weeks ago, Mom would have freaked out if a girl had come over at all, much less more than once. But Mom's attitude had undergone a little magical adjustment therapy, and now she had turned into some kind of "cool mom." It was kind of scary.

Lizzie came upstairs with Dodger trailing invisibly behind her and threw three rolled-up posters on the bed. "They're ruined," she said in disgust.

"What do you mean, ruined?"

"They're blue—all blue. One hundred percent blue. Apparently Dodger's camera only takes blue pictures."

"Uh, can I see them anyway?" I asked.

I could tell Lizzie didn't even want to see the posters again, but Dodger grabbed one right up. "Dude," he said, "I think they're pretty cool. I mean, come on—what's better looking than blue? That's right—nothing!" He opened the poster with a flourish.

And there I was, leaning against the blue tree with one hand, all decked out in the baseball uniform. Sure enough, I was blue. But I could see Dodger's point. The effect was kind of cool. Dodger laid that poster gently on the bed and then showed me the second one. I was wearing a suit, standing tall and straight in front of the late-afternoon sun. I thought I looked pretty mature and noble. Also, unfortunately, blue. The third poster was the best: me, back in my regular old jeans and T-shirt, with my backpack on one shoulder. Dodger put that poster down next to the other two just as Amy charged into my room unannounced. The girl was developing some alarmingly bad little-sister habits. On the other hand, she had kicked Beeks that morning. Maybe she was on my side.

Amy looked at the posters and snorted. "Hey, big brother. Are you running for President or Blueberry Princess? 'Cause if you're running for Blueberry Princess, your campaign is really getting good!"

She bent over one of the pictures, snatched up yet another blue hair for her evidence collection, and walked out. All right—even if she had kicked Beeks—she might not have been totally devoted to my campaign.

Lizzie, Dodger, and I all looked at one another. Then Lizzie and Dodger spoke at the same time. She said, "Sorry about the waste of time, Willie. We'll just have to—" And then he said, "So, bud, am I right or am I right? I say we go blue all the—"

I cut them both off by jumping up and shouting, "THAT'S IT! Dodger, you're a genius!"

Once again, I heard two voices at once. Dodger said, "I am?" Lizzie said, "He is?" Then he said, "Wait, I'm not?" and looked at Lizzie with puppy-dog eyes. I mean, puppy-dog eye. Well, puppy-chimp eye. Anyway, she replied, "I'm sorry, Dodger. I didn't mean—it's just that you're rather—"

"QUIET!" I yelled. "We're not throwing out the posters, Lizzie! I know exactly what they need to say. We're going to use these posters. In fact, we're going to print up a whole bunch of them. And we're going to win this election, fair and square!"

CHAPTER SIX

Take Your Pick

LIZZIE, DODGER, AND I had a lot of work to do that night, but we got it done together. The next morning, for the third day in a row, I was the first kid at school. Lizzie was right behind me (Dodger was at home, sleeping in his lamp on my top shelf). Lizzie and I each carried a big roller tube of posters and a tape gun. By the time the front doors of the building opened, we had plastered the hallways and classroom doors with our posters. There were equal numbers of posters with each picture, but all of them had my name across the top and the same slogan across the bottom. They said:

VOTE FOR WILLIE RYAN
THE TRUE-BLUE CANDIDATE

When the last piece of tape was stuck to the last wall, Lizzie smiled at me, and I gave her a high five. Then we leaned against the lockers and watched the students come in. People were stopping to read the posters, pointing at them, giving us little thumbs-up signs. I saw Craig walk in and read a poster. He actually looked kind of impressed. Then James stepped through the door, pushed Craig aside, and scowled at my picture. He even reached out to rip the poster off the wall, but then—out of nowhere—Amy was next to him. She stamped on his toes, pushed him away from the poster, and stomped off down the hall.

Little sisters. You never know whether to hate them or give them a medal.

In class, Mrs. Starsky announced that we would be doing a whole mini-unit on elections: "Because it's great to see you all so excited about democracy in action!" I swear, the woman could turn anything into a lesson. I think if the classroom ceiling collapsed on her, she'd be lying on the floor with a hole in her head, going, "This is great, class! Now we can study how blood circulates through the human body!"

Apparently the highlights of the unit were going to be an assembly with speeches by each presidential candidate, and then another assembly with a second set of speeches, this time by the vice presidential candidates. And the first assembly would be in only five days. Assuming I survived that, the second one would be two days after that, with the election one day later.

Jeepers. Making posters was one thing, but standing in front of the whole entire school and sounding like I knew what the heck I was talking about? That was a whole new level of terror. I could feel the nervous sweat of failure pouring out of me already—at this rate, I might drown before I ever had a chance to speak. I couldn't wait to get home so I could thank Dodger for getting me into this mess. Lizzie, on the other hand, was squirming in her seat with joy. I knew I was lucky to have her help, but did she have to look so DELIGHTED about it?

At lunch, all Lizzie could talk about were the assemblies. She babbled on about "issues," "priorities," and the electoral whatchamacallit thing, while I looked around the cafeteria and tried not to run out of there screaming in total panic. I wondered how Beeks and Flynn were taking this new development, but I couldn't see them anywhere . . . until the last minute or so of lunch period, when they suddenly appeared against the back wall. Craig looked kind of nervous, but James was pounding him on the back and holding out his hand for a high five.

Uh-oh.

As soon as the bell rang, I found out why Beeks was so happy. There were new posters in the hallway. They featured side-by-side photos of him and me. Beeks was posing in front of the school, with his body facing the camera and his head turned to one side. He looked like a superhero. And the picture of me—YIKES! I was facing the camera, and it looked like I had my index finger up my nose. Beneath the pictures, in bright red letters, were these words:

BEEKS OR RYAN?
TAKE YOUR PICK!

My mind was churning. As the whole darn fifth grade rushed by me, pointing and laughing, I thought back. How in the world had Beeks gotten that picture? I was pretty sure I'd have remembered if someone had come up to me with a camera and said, "Okay, Willie. Stick your finger up your nostril and say CHEESE!" And then it hit me: the girl at the doughnut table. When she had told me about the chocolate on my lip, it had been a setup. She had taken the picture on her cell phone camera.

Holy cow. Dodger had been right about the lesson of *The Little Mermaid*. I should have been on the lookout for suspiciously helpful witches.

The afternoon was horrible. Everywhere I went, kids were pointing, staring, and cracking up in my face. My class passed Amy's on the way to art class, and she whispered to me, "What are they all laughing about? If you ask me, 'snot funny at all!" Then she giggled. "'Snot funny! Get it?"

61

Yeah, I got it, Sherlock.

After school, Lizzie grabbed my elbow when we got off the bus and marched me toward my house. "What's going on?" I asked.

Through gritted teeth, she said, "Crisis meeting." She steamrolled me into my house, right past my parents, and up to my room. As soon as we got there, she strode over and banged three times on the side of Dodger's lamp.

He appeared beside it, in bright orange pj's. He was wearing an old-fashioned nightcap and clutching his ears. "Lizzie, OWW! What's going on?" he asked.

I looked at her. "Yeah, that's what *I* said."

Lizzie explained the whole poster thing to Dodger. I couldn't bear to hear it again, so I ran downstairs to get a snack. My dad was sitting in the big chair in our living room and asked me, "Son, is your friend up there talking to herself?"

"Dad," I said with what I hoped was a light-hearted tone, "that's silly. Why would Lizzie be talking to herself?"

Great. Now Amy was investigating us, my mom was practically planning our wedding, and my father thought Lizzie was a nutcase. I trudged back up to my room, where Dodger was sitting on my bed. He still had on his bizarre sleeping outfit, but was holding a pencil and a writing pad. Lizzie was using the dry-erase board in my room to give him a lecture. And—get this—Dodger was taking notes!

Then, out of nowhere, I heard the weirdest music. It sounded as if there were a million percussion instruments going at once, but all of the instruments sounded like coconuts being banged against logs or something. There were singers, too—if you could call them that. They were chanting, "*Ook ook eeee eeee eeee, ook ook eeee eeee eeee,*" over and over in harmony. The effect was kind of amazing.

Lizzie said, "Dodger, what in the world is that?"

Looking around with exaggerated casualness, Dodger said, "Oh, that? It's just the Chimptopian National Anthem. Technically, we should stand up right now, eat a banana, and scratch under our—"

"No, I mean, where is it coming from?"

He started edging his way toward the shelf that held his lamp. "Uh, it's just my ring tone. But don't worry, I didn't use my cell phone to call any old magical friends or anything, because I'm not at all

worried that you'll get totally slaughtered in the—
I mean, I wouldn't just go calling the Great—uh,
let me just take this call, okay? Back in a jiffy!"

With a snap of his long fingers, Dodger disappeared into the lamp. The jungle music stopped. Lizzie and I were left to stare at each other in horror. Very quietly she asked, "Did Dodger just say what I think he said?"

"I'm not sure. What do you think he said?"

"What do you think I think he said?"

"I think you think he—oh, never mind! I think he said he called the Great Lasorda. But he couldn't possibly be that dumb, could he?"

Lizzie looked at me some more without another word. But the scrunched-up look on her face told me everything I needed to know. And that was some scary news. See, the Great Lasorda was this superpowerful genie who was Dodger's boss for thousands of years. And I had accidentally freed Dodger from working for Lasorda when I wished for Dodger to be my best friend forever. There was this fire in my kitchen and some really burned salmon and a baseball game. Oh, and a bunch of magic.

Hey, if you think that all sounds pretty complicated, you should have tried living through it. And if Lizzie and I were right, I had a feeling my life was about to get complicated again.

Yeah, like it wasn't already.

After a few minutes, Dodger popped out of his lamp with a sheepish grin on his face. "Well," he said, "that was interesting. It seems my dear aunt Sally has been growing mujango beans in her rainforest garden again this fall. And little Cousin Bongo is getting his vine-swinging license. It's always nice to catch up with the old—what? What are you both staring at?"

"Dodger," Lizzie asked, advancing on him, "did you call the Great Lasorda today?"

"Um, well, that wasn't the Great Lasorda on the phone just now, I swear. It was just, uh, someone else."

I gave Dodger my best raised-eyebrow look (which I have to admit, I learned by watching Amy). "For real?"

Dodger put his hand over his chest. "Cross my heart and hope to smell a durian fruit!"

"What the heck, Dodger?"

Lizzie chimed in, "You know, a durian fruit. They're considered a delicacy in Southeast Asia, but are famed for their unpleasant—"

"I don't care about the stupid fruit, Lizzie. I want to know what the heck he was doing on the phone if he wasn't talking to Lasorda."

"Buddy, it was no biggie, okay? I was just talking to, uh, a member of my family. So, Lizzie," Dodger said, "can you get back to telling me about your three-part election strategy?" He smiled dazzlingly at her. "I love hearing all of your clever plans!"

Lizzie fell for it—she totally let Dodger distract her from whatever trouble he had been creating on the phone. I swear, she's willing to argue with me at an instant's notice, but she instantly forgets her brains for the first flattering chimp that comes along and flashes some teeth her way.

Girls!

Well, at least I would get to hear Lizzie's brilliant ideas. Apparently, our campaign should address three topics, which Mrs. Starsky had explained while I was staring out the classroom window and panicking. The topics were school climate, school rules, and school spirit. So we needed to come up with intelligent things to say about each of them. Lizzie stood next to the dry-erase board, chewing on the closed cover of a marker, waiting for our input.

I was wracking my brains, trying to come up with something that sounded like a president might say it, when Dodger jumped straight up in the air and shouted, "I've got it! I've got it!"

Lizzie was so startled that she accidentally bit down on the cap of the marker, splitting it in half. She got a mouthful of bright blue ink and ran out of the room gagging. I ran after her, while Dodger hid himself in my closet. Lizzie ran into the bathroom and slammed the door behind her. Of course this was the perfect moment for Amy to appear, so she came out of her room, chewing a huge wad of gum. She walked around me, Sherlock Holmes–style deerstalker cap on her head, and examined me with her magnifying glass. I didn't say a word; I just hoped Amy might finish checking me out and go away before Lizzie came back out.

No such luck. Amy turned away from me and knocked on the bathroom door.

"Ick 'er'a'ent!" Lizzie exclaimed.

"What?" I asked.

"Ick 'er'a'ent!"

Amy put one hand on her hip and used the other to poke me in the chest with her magnifying glass. "What in the world does that mean, Willie? Did you guys come up with some kind of dorky president code just so I wouldn't be able to solve your campaign secrets? Come on, you can tell me—I'm your sister! What does 'ick 'er'a'ent! mean?"

"I don't know, I swear! Lizzie, are you okay? What does 'ick 'er'a'ent! mean?"

The door burst open, and Lizzie was standing there with a fluorescent blue stain all around her mouth. When she opened her mouth to yell at me, I saw that her teeth and tongue were blue, too. "It's permanent, you goofball!"

I started to apologize and tell Lizzie that I didn't think that particular brand of marker caused *permanent* stains, but Amy started talking first. "Well, jeepers, Lizzie, you could have just said so!"

The next thing I knew, Lizzie was running out of the house.

Amy was still standing next to me on the top of the landing. She blew a bubble, cracked it loudly, and said, "God! I hope when *I* meet the boy *I'm* going to marry, *I'm* not so obnoxious to *him*!"

CHAPTER SEVEN

The Skater Walk and the Secret Life of Craig Flynn

HALF AN HOUR LATER, Dodger and I were sitting glumly on the edge of my bed. I had called
Lizzie's house, but her mom said she didn't want to
talk. I couldn't stand it. I knew I had to be careful
about talking with Dodger because Amy was prowl-
ing around, so I blasted some music. Then my mom
came up, knocked, came in, sat next to me, and
asked me to turn it down. Before her magical adjustment, Mom would have given me a whole big
lecture on the horrors of popular music, but now
she just mussed my hair and said, "Arguing with a

girl, then cranking up the tunes—my Willie is turning into a teenager!"

After she walked out, Dodger started jumping around, saying, "My Willie is turning into a teenager! My Willie is turning into a teenager!" and laughing his head off. Boy, was he a riot. And had my mother actually used the phrase "cranking up the tunes"?

Dodger said, "Whoa, little teenage dude! I have the BEST idea. I've been thinking—for the election, you know?—that you need a cooler walk. I mean, no offense, but you need a cool-kid stride, a manly strut. Buddy, you need a skater walk! Now would be the perfect time to get you one. And then when you go grooving your way up to the stage for your speech, everybody will know what I know—that Willie Ryan is the most awesome presidential-type guy around!"

"Uh, Dodger? How do I get a new walk? I mean, I walk the way I walk. That's just how I am."

"Nah, that's how you *think* you are. Listen, I once had this really weird gig on a ship, helping this Greek guy named Jason find a golden fleece, and—"

"What the heck is a golden fleece?"

"It's like a fur coat made of gold, but that's not the point. The point is that I was sailing around for, like, a year. And when I got back onto land, my whole stride was totally different. For like a century after that, the Great Lasorda used to imitate my walk and call me his "little sailor monkey.""

"Oh, so all I have to do is sail around the world a few times, and then I'll have a walk that even a genie with sparkly gold pants can feel free to laugh at?"

"No, that's just how I did it. You don't need a sailor walk anyway. And getting a skater walk should be a lot easier."

"All right, I'm listening. How do I get a skater walk?"

"Easy. All you have to do is learn to FLY!"

Oh, swell. All I needed to do was learn to *fly*. Why hadn't I thought of that before?

Half an hour later, I was in the woods with Dodger, wearing my bike helmet and a look of utmost fear. Dodger was trying to get me to step onto the Magic Carpet of Khartoum. He was also trying to persuade me to lose the helmet.

What's the Magic Carpet of Khartoum? Apparently, it's a flying carpet, just like in the Aladdin stories, but even scarier—because when you're on the Magic Carpet of Khartoum, you're totally invisible! So anyway, Dodger said, "Bud, I'm telling you: There's totally no point to wearing the helmet. You want to hear the wind whistling through the fur on your ears! Besides, it's not like the helmet will do any good. You're not going to fall, and if you did—well—I don't think the helmet would really save you from—oh, never mind. Like I said, you're not going to fall."

With those words of comfort ringing in my ears, I listened to Dodger's very helpful instructions on proper flying-carpet usage. Here are some tips, for those of you who might want to try this at home with your own airborne floor coverings:

-Dude, you've totally got to BE the carpet.

-The carpet is, like, your friend.

-All you have to do is—well, you just lean the way you want to go, and the carpet pretty much—I mean, usually— the carpet kind of just does it.

-Don't look down. Remember: The carpet is totally in-
visible, so you REALLY don't want to look down.

-Don't hit any power lines. Seriously . . . don't.

-Oh, and tree limbs really hurt. I mean, duh! They're
completely made of wood.

-Since you're invisible, you can't see your feet. And since
the carpet is invisible, you can't see the edge. I strongly
advise you to, like, not move your feet around.

-Remember the "don't look down" part. And the thing
about the power lines.

-Have fun!

Then Dodger decided I was ready for a test-
drive. He got on the carpet (which, of course, I
couldn't even see . . . but I could tell he'd gotten on
it when I suddenly couldn't see *him*) and told me to
stand behind him with my arms around his waist.
Stepping on was unbelievable. I mean, everyone
probably has dreams of being invisible, but when it
really happens, your brain just can't handle it. I
kept thinking, *Ahhh! Where's my hand? Where are my*
feet? And this was the weirdest part of all—because
I'd never even realized I could always see it at the

lower inside edge of my vision—*WHERE'S MY NOSE?*

Eventually I got over this enough to function, and Dodger talked to me until I followed his voice and found his waist. This was odd, too. My face felt the sensation of being pressed up against Dodger's furry back, but I was looking right through him at the view ahead.

"Ready, buddy?" Dodger asked.

"Uh, wait, I'm not really—"

"All right, then. Dude, let's FLY!"

So we did. Holy moley! I can't even come close to telling you what it was like, but I'll try. Picture the scariest roller coaster you've ever been on, with no safety harness. I mean, I hate roller coasters with a burning passion—but this was the single coolest thing that had ever happened to me. We were flying low over the trees, passing birds in midair. Dodger was leaning to one side, then the other, and we were banking from side to side, like a plane when it's turning to land. And the wind was whistling around my furry ears—well, at least, it was whistling through the holes in my helmet.

"Having fun?" Dodger shouted over his shoulder.

I wanted to scream or cry or just whimper. But amazingly, all that came out of my mouth was a big belly laugh. And once I started laughing, I couldn't stop. Dodger was laughing, too, so hard that I could feel his whole body shaking. "Hold on, dude," he said. "It's time for some advanced maneuvers!"

Let me tell you, if you've ever gone flying off a skateboard ramp, you might have some starting point for understanding Dodger's advanced maneuvers. Just picture that, but upside down, with some loop-de-loops thrown in. And you're invisible, fifty feet up, holding on desperately to an invisible chimp. Jeepers. I wasn't sure if I should have a heart attack or let go of Dodger, pound on my chest like King Kong, and shout my war cry to the skies.

I settled for laughing some more. In fact, I didn't stop until Dodger said, "Sssshhhhh! We have to be quiet now! Look!"

I hadn't really been paying attention to the view below me, especially since Dodger had told me specifically not to look down. But when I did, I couldn't believe it. We were over the school playground. Directly below us, James Beeks and Craig

Flynn were sitting on the swing set, having an argument. Dodger drifted lower and lower until we were hovering between two sets of tube slides, maybe twenty feet away from the swings. I could hear James saying: "We have to win. Ryan and Barrett embarrassed me publicly. They challenged me. Dude, they challenged *us*."

Flynn nodded. "That's true," he said. "But you were getting in their faces first. Besides, what do you have against them anyway?"

"I just hate the way stupid Ryan ruined my whole baseball season."

Craig frowned. "How did he ruin your season? He got the big game-tying hit in the championship, right?"

James snarled, "But then we lost anyway in extra innings. And I made the last out! All season long, I got the big hits. All season long, Willie Ryan struck out. I mean, come on—there's a reason why we called him Wimpy all year. Then the one time he gets a hit, my dad is there, and—"

Craig said, "I still don't get it. What does his hit have to do with you?"

James said, "Duh. You know my dad only came

to that one game all stupid season, right? And I had to blow the game in front of him. And then when I got off the field, Ryan was standing right next to us, and *both* of his parents were giving him a hug. Then that ugly Lizzie gave him a high five. Meanwhile my father looked over at Wimpy and said, 'Too bad you're not a clutch hitter like that kid James!'"

Neither one of them said anything for a while. Then Craig said, "I'm sorry that happened to you, but I still don't see the big deal about the election."

"Craig, this is my big chance to show my dad I'm a winner again. And that's why we have to sneak back into that school and—"

"I won't do it, James. I won't cheat!"

"What are you talking about, Craig? You cheat all the time. Remember when you got busted for copying off Wimpy's spelling test? What was that, an accident?"

"No, but that was different. If I had gotten a better grade on that, it wouldn't have made someone else get a lower grade. But if we cheat on this and win, it hurts Lizzie and Willie."

"And what do you care?"

"Umm . . . well . . . I don't know. But there's another thing, too. My mom said if I get in trouble at school one more time, she's going to take away my cell phone."

"And?'

"James, you know this. Don't you even listen when I tell you stuff?"

"Kind of."

Craig snorted. "You know my mom's been divorced twice. And you know my ex-stepdad has custody of my little half brother every other week."

"Yeah, and?"

"Well, my brother, Tyler, gets nightmares. So I sleep with my cell phone on vibrate under my pillow. And when he gets really scared, Tyler calls me."

Wow, I couldn't believe it! Craig Flynn—big, scary Craig Flynn—was, like, his little brother's protector.

James made a face and said, "Aww . . . that's tho thweet! Cwaig helps his wittle bwother!"

"Oh, shut up. The point is, I can't get caught— wait! What's that?"

Craig was pointing right at us!

"What's what?" James asked.

Dodger said, "Oopsie! I need to take evasive action. Hold on!"

Wow, I thought advanced maneuvers had been wild, but evasive action opened up a whole new world of heart-stopping panic. First we shot straight up maybe thirty feet. Then we rocketed backward into the trees at the edge of the playground so fast that I thought my nose would break against Dodger's shoulder blade. Finally we did a full 180-degree-spin move, then accelerated to absolute top speed as Dodger . . . umm . . . dodged his way between the tree trunks until we shot out of the woods into my backyard.

Then we stopped so short that we went tumbling off the front of the carpet together. I think I might have fainted for a moment, but when I opened my eyes, Dodger was smiling from ear to ear. "Oh, man," he said. "That was *awesome*!"

I felt like I had to swallow to keep my heart from flying up my throat and out my mouth. So I gulped a few times. Then I said, "What happened back there? I thought the carpet was invisible."

"Well, it is, mostly."

"What do you mean, mostly? How can some-thing be *mostly* invisible?"

"Dude," Dodger said. "Aren't *I* mostly invisible? I mean, nobody but you and Lizzie can see me."

Good point. "But wait, didn't Craig just see us? Oh, wow, I am so—"

"No, Craig couldn't see *us*. He must just be a Carpet Seer, that's all. It's not that crazy. I mean, there used to be a whole bunch of Carpet Seers in Roswell, New Mexico, and back in 1947, they saw me out on a practice run with—"

"What's a Carpet Seer?"

"Well, it's like having one of the minor magical subtalents. You know, like having the Ghost Ear. Or being a Horse Whisperer. Or an Elf Smeller."

Elf smeller? *Elf smeller?* "So, all these different kinds of people can see or feel or hear magic?"

Dodger looked thoughtful. "Willie, I think al-most all people could—if they gave it a chance."

Then the sparkle came back into Dodger's eye, and he yanked me to my feet. "Walk!" he com-manded.

My knees were pretty shaky, and it was weird seeing myself again. I kept feeling cross-eyed from staring at my own nose. But I had to admit, when I walked, there was a whole new roll to my steps. "Buddy," Dodger said, "you are looking *good*! I am a great flight instructor!"

That made me smile. But the next thing he said wiped the smile right off.

"In fact, I think you're ready to fly *solo*!"

CHAPTER EIGHT

Headaches and Handshakes

SO THAT'S WHY I went to school the next day with a black eye. It was pretty gruesome, and I don't really want to talk about it. All I will tell you—just in case you ever try to fly a magic carpet—is that the hard part is avoiding both power lines *and* tree trunks at the SAME TIME. Oh, and if your mom ever has to pull many shreds of bark out of your cheek and eyebrow with tweezers, tell her to be gentle with the rubbing alcohol.

Trust me.

Even though I was mortified at the thought of

seeing anyone, I marched right to the school bus stop in the morning. My mom said that black eyes usually look even worse the second day, so it would be no use staying home, plus I had to tell Lizzie about the discussion between James and Craig. And I wanted to know if she was still mad at me for the problem with the marker, even though it totally hadn't been my fault.

I got to the bus stop before her. Amy walked there with me but stayed about ten feet to my left—I don't think she wanted to be seen with her black-and-blue, alleged nose picker of a brother. I had my baseball cap on, pulled way down so the shadow of the bill covered the top half of my face. When Lizzie got there, she stood about ten feet to my right. I noticed she had a scarf wrapped around the entire bottom half of her face.

We looked like some sort of demented cosmic twins. I forced myself to stroll casually over to her with my cool new skater walk, took a deep breath, and pushed my hat way back on my forehead. Lizzie gasped and said through several layers of scarf, "Oh, my goodness! What on earth happened to your eye? And why are you limping?"

Hmm. Maybe the skater walk still needed a tune-up. I said, "Long story. How's your mouth?"

She looked both ways to make sure nobody was around, and unwrapped herself. It was my turn to gasp. She looked like her lips had been attacked by blind face painters. Sloppy blind face painters. I said, "It's all right. It doesn't really look... that..." And then I couldn't help myself. I let out a little giggle. I covered my mouth, horrified at the thought that now Lizzie would hate me forever. But then she started giggling, too. By the time the bus pulled up, my hat was completely off, her scarf was in her coat pocket, and we were laughing so hard we had to hold on to each other to keep from falling over.

That's when James's cheerleader friend opened her bus window, held up her cell phone, and took their next campaign picture.

We got on the bus, and Lizzie kept asking me how I'd gotten the black eye. Of course, the entire busload of kids was staring at us, so I told her I'd explain the whole thing later. At lunch, when we were seated at our usual table away from everybody else, Lizzie decided that "later" had arrived.

After a whole morning of being teased about the eye without being able to tell anyone how it had happened, I was ready to talk.

I gave Lizzie the story in great detail, and her eyes just lit up. When I was finished, she asked, "What did you tell your parents when you got home? And what did they say?"

"I told them I had fallen off my bike trying to jump a ramp in the woods. You know my mom isn't nearly as protective as she used to be, but she was pretty mad about that. Plus, of course, my glasses got pretty bent up, which always makes her mad. While she was cleaning up my face, she made me promise like a thousand times that I wouldn't try any more jumps."

"And your dad? What did he say?"

"Well, he just sat there quietly while Mom was giving me the lecture. Then, when she left the bathroom, he leaned over and asked me, 'So, was it *cool*?' "

Lizzie laughed, but then she got all serious and said, "So, was it? Because—because—WOW! You FLEW!"

I shushed her frantically, but the roar of the

lunchroom appeared to have prevented the others from hearing her. "Uh, it was kind of cool," I admitted.

Lizzie said, "I knew it! So can I go flying with you?"

"No," I said. "Absolutely not. It's too dangerous."

Lizzie said, "Oh, Willie! Are you trying to protect me? That's really sweet!"

Jeepers.

Then she stamped her foot under the table and said, "But if *you* can do it, *I* can do it!"

Double jeepers.

I didn't know what to say. I really didn't want Lizzie to get hurt. Heck, I didn't want *me* to get hurt; the very thought of climbing back on that carpet made my stomach feel all funny. But, on the other hand, if she had gone flying on a magic carpet without me, I'd be absolutely dying to go, too. I got a break from replying when James and Craig appeared in the doorway of the cafeteria. James was cracking up, but Craig definitely looked annoyed.

Swell.

The bell rang, and the whole grade got its

newest episode of campaign entertainment. I had no idea how they had done it so fast, but James and Craig had put up a new set of posters. These featured side-by-side photos again. On the left, James and Craig were standing solemnly in front of an American flag, which was blowing majestically in the wind. On the right, Lizzie and I were huddled together, bruised and stained. The caption on this one said:

RED, WHITE, AND BLUE
or BLACK AND BLUE?
TAKE YOUR PICK!

Grr.

As soon as we got to class, Mrs. Starsky called James into the hallway. My seat is right in front by the door of our classroom, and when we got back up there, I could hear Mrs. Starsky arguing that James would have to take the posters down. She told him they were cruel, and that this was his second mean poster in a row. He said, *But in the last election, the Republican candidates insulted each other's religions.* I had to admit, he had a point. She told him the posters were unacceptable. He said, *But in America we have freedom of speech. And aren't these elections supposed to teach us about American values?* Ooh, I had to admit, he was *good*. She accused him and Craig of sneaking out of the lunchroom to use the school's computer lab to make the posters. He said, *W-e-e-l-l-l-l-l* . . . She warned him that if she caught them sneaking around the building again, there would be serious consequences. He assured her it wouldn't happen again, and the posters stayed up.

By the next day, Lizzie's mouth was pretty much back to normal, but my eye had turned the sickly blackish green of a rotting banana peel. Also, it was throbbing pretty constantly. Maybe that's why my speech didn't turn out so great. This was my first draft:

Dear fellow classmates,

Hi, I'm Willie Ryan. I am running for fifth-grade president, and my running mate is Lizzie Barrett. She's running for vice president. We are supposed to talk about three things: school environment, school rules, and school spirit. I like our school environment. If I become president, I would like it even better because I would be president of it. I think our school would have a better environment if the teachers bought nice plants for their windows. I think I would be good at getting teachers to buy plants. Plants make oxygen, and I like oxygen. So do you, I bet.

About those rules: I think it should be a rule that lunch is longer. With recognizable meats. And there should be no tests on Fridays or Mondays. Possibly not ever. On the other hand, Lizzie likes tests. I'll see what I can do.

On the topic of school spirit, I have a lot of school spirit. Just the other day I wore a school sweatshirt to school, which showed a lot of spirit. Also, my favorite pencil has our school's name on it.

So please vote for me and Lizzie. We are true blue. Also, we are not geeks. James was just saying that.

I read the speech to Lizzie at my house after school. She said it was all wrong. "First of all," she said in her snotty, perfect British-girl tone, "you don't say 'My fellow classmates.' It's redundant, because your classmates are automatically your fellows. Also, blah blah blah . . ."

I mean, she didn't actually say blah blah blah. It's just that after a while, that's what I heard. Of course, we argued about it. She said she'd rewrite it for me, and I said I could do it myself. Then she said I was stubborn and ungrateful. I said I just didn't want a vice president who told me what to do all the time. She said that I shouldn't worry, because all I had to do was give that speech, and I'd definitely lose the election and not *have* a vice president, period.

The argument got so bad that Dodger woke up from his mid-afternoon nap under my bed and scolded us. "Dudes," he said, "you're, like, total pals. Don't let some stupid election make you forget that, all right?" Then he made us shake hands, which was completely embarrassing. Especially because my palm was all sweaty. I swear, I wasn't nervous about shaking hands with Lizzie or anything. It was just really hot in the house. In fact, it was so hot I needed a drink. I went downstairs, got juice boxes for us, and went back up.

Lizzie and Dodger looked way too happy when I got there. I said sheepishly, "Okay, Lizzie, do you want to help me fix up my speech now?" Dodger did his weird one-eyed wink thing and said, "No worries, Willie. It's, like, taken care of."

"Uh, hold on a minute. What do you mean, it's taken care of?"

Dodger held up my speech. "I mean, this is totally out of your hands, dude. Just leave this speech in the hands of the expert!"

"Expert? What kind of expert are you?"

He rolled his eye. "What kind of expert am I? A speech expert, that's what kind of expert. Did you ever hear of a guy named Thomas Jefferson? Who wrote a little thing called the Declaration of Independence?"

This was too much, even for Dodger. "Are you telling me you helped Thomas Jefferson write the Declaration of Independence?"

Dodger said, "Well, not exactly. I was, like, supposed to. But then that Ben Franklin guy tricked me into holding some kite with a key on it—and by the time I woke up, I'd missed the whole revolution. Which was really too bad for George Washington, because I made him this really awesome set of magic teeth, and I never even got to give them to him. The Great Lasorda ended up selling the teeth to some boxer named Muhammad something or other, like, two hundred years later, and they made him float like a butterfly and sting like a bee. But that's not even the point. The point is, I was totally ready to write that whole declaration, just like I'm totally ready to make your speech the best one ever!"

I said, "Um, I totally appreciate the offer and all, but I'd really rather just do the whole thing myself if you don't mind." I reached for the paper.

There was a POOF! Suddenly Dodger was gone. So was Lizzie. So was the speech.

Just then, Amy knocked on the door. When I opened it, she was wearing her Sherlock clothes and was carrying a stethoscope my parents had gotten her for her fifth birthday, when she was going through her "I want to be a puppy doctor" phase. "A-ha!" she exclaimed. "Entering the suspect's room, I find one boy—where only moments ago I heard three voices. I'm going to solve this mystery, or my name isn't Sherlock Holmes!"

"Uh, no offense, Amy, but your name ISN'T Sherlock Holmes."

She kicked me in the shin. All of a sudden, I

felt kind of sorry for James Beeks. And anyone who would ever have to face Amy on a soccer field. "By the way," she said, "I agree with Lizzie and the mysterious, unseen character with the deep voice. Your speech needs some serious work."

CHAPTER NINE

A Little Help from My Friends

"WILLIE, IT'S A DISASTER!" Lizzie shouted as she came charging up to the bus stop on Monday morning.

"What are you talking about? Where did you and Dodger disappear to? And what's the disaster? Are you okay? Is Dodger all right?"

She said, "Dodger's fine, and I'm fine. We flew on the magic carpet. It was brilliant! Dodger told me I was a much better carpet pilot than—I mean, he said I was a natural."

Oh, so Lizzie was a better carpet pilot than I

was, huh? Super. "So, Miss Flying Ace, what's the problem?"

"The problem is where Dodger said he was going after he dropped me off."

Dear Reader, here's some more life advice from your friend Willie:

-If your two best friends, one of whom has access to magical objects, suddenly disappear right after telling you not to worry about it, do yourself a favor: Worry about it.

-If one of those friends tells the other one he's "just popping into the school to fix something," worry about it even more.

-If the other friend gets all cocky about her ability to fly one of those magical objects, try really hard not to slug her.

"What do you mean, after he dropped you off? Maybe you should just tell me the whole story from the beginning."

Fortunately, the bus was late, because this story was a doozy. "Well," Lizzie said, "it started when we left your room, obviously. We reappeared in the Field of Dreams, and Dodger explained the whole flying thing to me. But he told me that if he let me fly, I would owe him a favor later. And I had to give my word of honor. That was tricky. I mean, I trust that Dodger means well, but his ideas— well, you know."

Yeah, I knew exactly what she meant.

"I gave him my word, though. I mean, a friend is a friend, right? Plus, I admit it: I really wanted to fly. So he gave me the basics, and those were so easy that pretty soon I was doing an Ollie over the town water tower—you know, like in skateboarding, when you push down on the back of your board and do a little jump? I'm sure Dodger showed you that one, it's so elementary. Anyway, while you were doing your Ollie over the water tower, did Dodger tell you the origin of the term? My next-door neighbor's older brother is big into skateboarding, and he once told me that Ollie was short for *allez-oop*, which is what French circus performers used to shout before leaping into the air. But Dodger informed me that it really comes from Ali

Baba. Apparently, Dodger was once showing him how to fly over the pyramids in Egypt and—"

"Listen," I said gruffly. I was kind of hurt that Dodger had taught Lizzie more than he had taught me, but I didn't want to tell her that. "Can we just get on with the story?"

"Sure, but you don't have to be so snappish about it. I don't see why you should get to do all the cool magical stuff while I just sit in my room and—"

I cleared my throat forcefully.

"Okay, okay. So after I mastered the Ollie maneuver, Dodger asked me to identify the worst weaknesses of your speech so he could fix them. We were doing some Immelman turns, which are just *so* dead easy, and—"

"Wait, can you back up a minute?"

"Immelman turns, Willie, don't you remember? When you do half of a vertical loop in the air, then flip back right-side up?"

"No, I don't care about the turns. What was the thing about the speech?"

"Oh, that. I told him I thought the biggest flaw was your atrociously simple vocabulary. It was weird. He said, 'Right, vocabulary. That's what I thought. Perfect!' Then he took control of the carpet, swooped across half the town in one steep dive, practically crash-landed in my backyard, and said, 'Wow, look, we're at your house already! Gotta go! See you tomorrow—I've got to go see a guy about some fancy words!' The next thing I knew, he was gone. You know what this means, don't you?"

"Uh, that my best friends think I'm a moron?"

"No, Willie, think for a minute. As far as I know, Dodger only knows one vocabulary expert. He told us that he'd been on the phone with a member of his family, right?"

"Yeah, so?"

"So you've met a member of Dodger's family, right? A blue chimp who sounded like a walking thesaurus?"

Jeepers, I couldn't believe it. For better or for worse, Lizzie was right about one thing: Dodger's brother, Rodger, had to be back in town. Which was weird, because for a while there I had thought that Dodger and Rodger might be the same person. Chimp. Whatever. The bus finally pulled up to our stop, and the conversation ended. When we got to our seats, Lizzie wanted to put our heads close together and whisper some more about the situation, but I made a big show of busting out with my music player and popping in my earbuds. I knew I was being kind of obnoxious to her, but I just didn't want to hear any more about what a great, smart flier she was.

It was the day before the big speech assembly, but nobody said anything to me all day about the election. James just sat at his desk smirking, like he was already planning his victory party, and Craig spent the day chewing his fingernails down to dirty, ragged stumps. Every time I looked at Lizzie, she was turning and tumbling her pencil through the air with a dreamy expression on her face. I suppose if my flying lesson hadn't ended up with me hugging a tree, maybe I would have kept reliving it, too.

When I got home, I had to go through a whole debriefing with my parents. Amy had clued them in about the election, and they were all pumped up about it. Here's what my mom had to say:

"Oh, William, we are so proud of you! You're just blossoming before our eyes. Just a few weeks ago, you were so timid that we actually worried you were too shy. But now—WOW! Our baby boy is a baseball star, an amateur stuntman, and now a handsome, dashing politician. And so modest, too. I can't believe you didn't tell us about this. Why, if Amy hadn't spilled the beans, we wouldn't have even known there was an election coming up. Oh, don't roll your eyes like that, Willie! Your sister is just so fascinated by the big-boy adventures of her older brother. She actually has a whole fantasy built up about a mysterious, deep-voiced campaign helper with BLUE HAIR, if you can believe that. It's just so cute! Anyway, if you need any help, just ask. I'm great at making posters, and you know your father is always looking for an excuse to get involved with your activities. And Amy tells me you have a speech to rewrite. You know, your father *does* write for a living."

Now, normally I refused to accept school help from my parents, because if I asked either of them the slightest question, my mom and dad each had a tendency to get totally obsessed with the assignment. I remember this one time I asked my dad to help me solve a math problem about time zones, and he spent the next several hours running around the house, bringing every watch, cell phone, and clock in the house to the dining room table, resetting them, and aligning them on a map of the world that he'd dug up from somewhere in the recesses of his huge rolltop desk. I didn't have the heart to tell him that there were, like, thousands of Web sites with detailed, live-action time-zone maps, or that I'd finished the homework before he even got all of the clocks downstairs.

But this time, I really needed the help, and my father actually was an expert in this field. So I sat down with him, and we worked on my speech for an hour. By the end, I was pretty proud of the work. Now all I had to do was stop Dodger and Rodger from ruining everything.

I thanked my dad and went up to my room. I closed the door behind me, turned on some music as an anti-Amy precaution, and said, "Dodger?" There was no answer. I rubbed his lamp, and he appeared beside me, groaning and covering his eyes.

"Dude," he said, "is it morning already? Man, we were up so late last night breaking into the—I mean, I was up so late, umm, reading comic books with—uh, myself. Yeah, reading. Alone. Because, well, that's how I read. Alone, I mean."

I raised an eyebrow. "So, you're saying you didn't go on any secret political missions last night? Missions that might have involved—oh, I don't know—a family member of yours?"

Dodger shifted his weight from foot to foot, looked everywhere but at me, and said, "Well . . ." His eyes flickered over to the lamp.

A-ha! I rubbed the lamp, and suddenly Dodger's brother, Rodger, was next to me, yawning. He was fully dressed in a pinstriped, dark blue suit, a very wrinkled white shirt, and a loosely knotted tie. His fur was sticking up in all directions. If you've never seen a chimpanzee with bed-head, it's really quite a spectacle. Especially if he starts talking to you while another chimp is jumping up and down nearby, frantically gesturing for him not to say anything.

"Hello, greetings, felicitations, Willie. It's good, satisfying, pleasurable to see you again. Honestly, when my brother, my sibling, my mother's other child called up the Great Lasorda and asked for help getting you elected, I thought the whole thing sounded like a recipe for disaster, a Titanic in the making, if you will. But the Master's plan was brilliant, sparkling, inventive. In fact, I think you will win the day, vanquish your foe, rise up to stunning new heights of—Willie, why are you staring at me in that strangely hostile manner? It's not every day that I break into a school, cast a magic vocabulary spell upon a speaking platform, and then settle down to a richly deserved slumber, only to be rudely awakened, tumbled out of the sleeping chamber, rousted by an ungrateful young—"

"BE QUIET!" I shouted. "What do you mean, you broke into my school and cast a spell on the podium? What did you do?"

Dodger was still jumping up and down next to me, making throat-slitting motions at Rodger. Fortunately it takes more than a direct threat to keep Rodger quiet. "You know," he said huffily, "you really shouldn't tell me to be quiet and then ask me two questions in the next breath. It creates a paradox, an oxymoron, a conundrum. Am I meant to obey your first instruction or accede to the demands that follow? Honestly, I can see why Dodger felt you needed communicative assistance. Anyway, the operation was quite ingenious. The Great

Lasorda gave me some enchanted dust that confers magical loquacity and instructed me to sprinkle it on the platform from which you are to speak, present, deliver your oration. In short, the next young person who gives a speech at that podium will sound exactly like me, myself, and I. All you have to do is speak first, and you will be just as splendidly well spoken as *I* am. Your classmates will love, adore, and admire you—and you will be sure to earn the coveted laurels of victory!"

Hoo boy.

CHAPTER TEN

The Old Switcheroo

AS I SAT ON STAGE in the school cafeteria-
auditorium the next morning in my wear-to-your-
cousin's-wedding suit, my hands were sweating so
much that the copy of my speech was all damp and
soggy. Lizzie was next to me, whispering, "Calm
down," every five seconds, even though nobody in
history has ever calmed down because someone
told them to. We were on one side of the podium,
and James sat with Craig on the other. The entire
student body was in front of us, and Dodger had
just appeared in back of the audience, holding a big
dry-erase board and a marker, but that wasn't what

had me so worked up. I was tormented by the thought of using magic to cheat on the speech, plus I wasn't so sure that sounding like Rodger would be an improvement. The Great Lasorda was a pretty shifty guy; maybe he wanted me to lose the election—in fact, the more I thought about it, the more sure I became that this whole magic-dust trick would backfire. And besides, now that my dad had gone over my speech with me, I thought it was pretty darn good.

Just as Mrs. Starsky gestured for me and James to approach the podium, I had an idea: I would leave things up to James. Mrs. Starsky had explained to me that he would choose who got to go first in this round of speeches, and I would decide the order in our second round. So when she made us shake hands, I whispered, "Hey, James, do you think maybe I could, um, go first? I mean, since you have the advantage and everything, being so well loved by everybody and all. Could you please just consider it?"

Lizzie looked over at me, and I could read her lips saying, *What are you doing?* I winked at her.

James pushed my hand away in disgust and

said, "Help you? Why would I help a dork like *you*?" Then he turned to Mrs. Starsky and put on a phony sweet-kid voice as he told her, "Ma'am, I think I'd like to go first today, all right?"

Lizzie's face suddenly lit up. I could tell she understood what had just happened. But Dodger wasn't going to be happy.

Mrs. Starsky nodded at James, wished us both luck, and stepped up to the podium. She leaned toward the microphone that was mounted on it, quieted everybody down, and gave James a big introduction. Way off in the distance, Dodger scribbled on the sign, "YU WER SUPPOSTA GO FURST!" A lot of the kids cheered when Mrs. Starsky said James's name, but a few sat with their arms crossed, looking unhappy. Maybe James didn't have quite as many friends as he thought.

James walked calmly to the platform, put his speech on the podium, and began. I could have sworn I saw some flashing sparkles in the air around his head as he spoke the first words, but maybe that was just my imagination. However, the disaster that followed was 100 percent real. Here, for the sake of historical accuracy, is a complete transcription of James Beeks's first presidential campaign speech:

Dear classmates, fellow students, comrades, peers, contemporaries,

I am here today to tell you the reasons, the whys and wherefores, the rationale to explain why I am the best, the greatest, the most deserving candidate in this election.

James paused at this point, squinted at his speech, picked up the pages, and shook them before continuing. Meanwhile, Dodger wrote: "O NO! HEEZ GONNA WINNN!"

You know I have always served in the student government of this school, this educational institution, this center of learning, to the best of my ability. And I think I have always done a good, great, exemplary, swell, fabulous, funky fresh, super-bad, righteous job.

James paused again, shaking his head as though he had water in his ear. Meanwhile, kids in the audience were starting to murmur, and a few giggles were breaking out around the room. Dodger erased frantically, then wrote: "SEE? WEER DED!"

So you have to ask yourself, wonder, ponder the issue of, decide whether you would rather have the most experienced man in office, or throw away, toss, waste your vote on [James pointed at me] this geek, this nerd, this dork, this loser, this pathetic, sniveling, chinless weakling.

Dodger jumped up and down, and pointed to his newest message: "NO CHIN? *DUDE!*" Meanwhile, Mrs. Starsky got up at this point and approached James. She did not look pleased. Mrs. Starsky whispered something in James's ear, and his whole face got pale.

Ahem, hrrm, hock-hock, gargle.

Wow, this was a powerful spell—it even made you clear your throat four different ways! Dodger stopped writing, looked puzzled for a moment, and then started to laugh.

Sorry, I just had something stuck in my throat, a bit of gooey phlegm, a wad of partially thickened mucus, a hocker, a loogie, a—

Students were openly turning away from James in disgust now, and there were definitely pockets of laughter around the room. Mrs. Starsky went up to James again, with what must have been a second warning. Dodger wrote: "HAY! THIS MITE BEE OK!"

Okay then, back to my speech, my monologue, my oration. I was saying that I should be president, leader, commander in chief of the armed forces, big kahuna, head honcho, silverback male of the school because of my experience. Also, I would like to thank Mrs. Starsky, this lady here, the massively boring woman to my left, she of the rancid coffee breath, and—"

"ENOUGH!" Mrs. Starsky roared, ripping the cord out of the microphone. Then, in front of the whole school, she screamed and yelled at James until he stormed off the stage. As he passed me, he hissed, "I don't know how you did this, but you are dead, deceased, extinct, six feet under, pushing up daisies! *This isn't over!*"

Boy, even if they get to go first, some people are just never satisfied.

After James stalked off, Mrs. Starsky plugged the microphone back in and introduced me. As I stood to approach the microphone, Lizzie whispered, "Good luck!" Dodger grabbed his marker again and wrote, "SK8ER WALK!" I gave it my best shot. At the podium, I looked out over the audience and tried to look serious and important. Dodger wrote, "SMILE!" So I did. Then he wrote, "NOT TWO MUCHHH!" I worked on smiling without smiling too much, took a deep breath, and gave my improved, polished speech. I don't know how much of it anyone actually heard, though, because the whole room was pretty much in an uproar. But at least I didn't make a fool out of myself. And if James had looked like a massive idiot—well, it had been kind of his choice. I mean, I almost could have felt a tiny bit sorry for him, but it wasn't like I had *told* him to go first or anything.

When we walked out of the auditorium, the

last thing I saw was Dodger's hands, reaching up over the crowd in a double V-for-victory sign.

For the rest of the day, people were talking about James's speech all over the school. Mrs. Starsky was flustered and grumpy; every time our class settled down, we could hear other teachers yelling at their classes to be quiet, and I kept hearing whispers and murmurs in the halls: *loogie . . . coffee breath . . . silverback male . . . hock . . . gargle . . .* I'm happy to say I didn't run into James or Craig all day, but then, on the way out to the bus lines, Lizzie and I saw them huddled together under the slides at the playground.

"Willie, come on!" Lizzie said, pulling on my arm. "We have to go listen to what they're saying."

I was horrified. "What do you mean? We can't just walk over there—Beeks will kill me! And it's not nice to sneak up and eavesdrop."

Lizzie looked a little embarrassed. She leaned against the school wall, pulled a dropper out of her coat, and used it to drip three drops of a brown, smelly liquid on the sole of each of her shoes. "I never got to finish telling you this the other day," she said, "but Dodger made me promise that the

113

next time I saw Craig and James talking, I should use this. It's called Tincture of Distraction, and while you're wearing it, nobody can concentrate on you unless they're in physical contact with you. It only works once on a pair of shoes, but it will let us sneak up on them without being noticed."

"And why do we want to do that?"

"Dodger told me that Craig needs help, and we're the only ones who can give it. The Great Lasorda told him so."

"But we don't trust the Great Lasorda. Plus, if he wants to help Craig so badly, why doesn't he just give the kid three wishes himself?"

"He can't," Lizzie said. "Craig is Irish."

"So what? I'm Irish, too," I replied.

"You're only half-Irish. Dodger said that, according to the Inter-Magical Cooperation Accords of 1817, only fully licensed leprechauns may help full-blooded Irish children with domestic problems. The Great Lasorda could get fined seventeen doubloons, a pint of pixie dust, and an ounce of myrrh if he interferes directly with Craig's family trouble."

"Myrrh? What the heck is myrrh?"

Lizzie gave me a pained look as she bent down to grab my right sneaker. "Does it matter, Willie? Craig needs our help, and I promised."

Sometimes it stinks being the good guys.

Lizzie started anointing my sneakers with the stinky stuff. The first one went fine, but she slipped a bit with the second one. "Oops," she said. "Oh, well—three drops, five drops, what's the difference?" I think maybe she's been hanging out with Dodger too much lately, if you want to know the truth. Anyway, then we tiptoed around the back of the playground and up the tube slide. From in there, we could hear every word Craig and James said, amplified by the plastic walls around us.

"James, I still don't understand what happened with the speech today."

"Craig, I already told you, I couldn't help myself. It was like I was a puppet or something. Somebody was *making* me say that stuff."

Craig didn't sound convinced. "You mean, like, they changed the words on your paper?"

"No, I mean they were controlling my brain! I wanted to read my speech the way it was written, but I just couldn't do it."

"Oh," Craig said. "So all we have to do is go to Mrs. Starsky and tell her that somebody was controlling your brain, and everything will be fine."

We heard a thwack, and Craig said, "OW! What did you do that for?"

"You idiot! Don't you know anything about politics?"

"Um, no. I don't. I'm only running for vice president because you told me to. You said I didn't need to know anything, that all I had to do is stand near you and look scary."

"Well, the first rule is that you never apologize for the truth. You make up a half-truth, deliver a half-apology, and then find a way to blame your opponent for the whole issue. It's called the weasel defense."

"Huh?"

"Listen: Let's say I had gas, okay?"

"Uh, okay. You had gas."

"Right. So I totally blasted one off, like, right in the middle of class. And then Willie Ryan made a face. Using the weasel defense, I'd say, 'Wow, did you hear that? Someone in this room has an innocent little tooting problem. I'm sorry for bringing this up, but my opponent doesn't seem to have any respect for our classmates who face physical challenges.' Then, whatever Ryan says, he looks like the bad guy."

Craig still had that doubting tone as he said, "And this *works*?"

"Are you kidding me? Have you ever listened to an election campaign? How many times did George W. Bush get elected? It's foolproof." We heard a thud and then some muffled, colorful language from Craig. "What's the matter, Craig? You just dropped your school bag; it's not like it's a big deal or anything."

Craig blurted, "Look, James! There are TWO cell phones in my bag. Not one, TWO!"

"Which means?"

"Which means my little brother forgot to take his phone with him to his dad's house, and then I accidentally threw it in my bag."

"So?"

"So, now when he wakes up in the middle of the night, he won't be able to call me."

"Okay, so you'll go home and tell your mom to drive you over there."

"I can't. She'll be at work, and there's no way my stepdad will drive me there. It's like twenty minutes each way. Plus, he hates seeing my *other* stepdad. Anyway, I can't tell them about my brother's night terrors, because then our mom won't let him go see his dad at all."

"Wow, sounds major."

"It *is* major, you jerk! Now my brother's going to be scared and alone, with nobody to—"

I could tell Craig really felt horrible. He might have been the toughest kid in the fifth grade (twice!), but he sure did have a soft spot for his brother. I started to wonder whether I would have been as worried if it had been Amy alone and scared in the dark. My thoughts were interrupted by a horrible burning sensation in my left big toe. It was hard to reach my foot, lying there in the tunnel, with Lizzie's feet in my face, but I managed. I ripped off my shoe, and in the dim reddish light coming through the plastic, I could see that the drops had eaten right through my sneaker and into my toe. I tried to check out the damage, but it was hard to focus my attention on the toe. I realized that the magic was spreading to my foot! Another wave of pain shot through me, and I winced. This made Lizzie slip. Her left knee whacked into my bruised cheekbone, and I dropped the sneaker. It clattered all the way down the slide, stopping with a resounding thump at the last turn.

James said, "Wait! What's that? Remember you thought you saw something here the other night? And then today something made me give that speech? I bet this place is haunted! I'm getting out of here!"

"Stop, James! What about my little brother? You're the smart one—you have to help me figure out what to do!"

At that moment, Lizzie shifted her weight in an attempt to get her knee out of my aching eye. We slipped about two feet down the slide with a shuffling, squeaky sound. James heard it and said, "Sorry, dude, but when it comes to ghosts, it's every man for himself! Later!" James's footsteps echoed as he charged away from the playground.

Lizzie and I were huddled together inside the slide, trying our hardest to disappear, when all of a sudden, a huge, steely hand closed around my bare foot, and Craig yanked me out the bottom of the slide.

CHAPTER ELEVEN

Geeks in Flight

"HEH, HEH. HI, CRAIG," I said. "We were just, uh—"

"About to die? Yeah, you were." Craig let go of my ankle, and I tumbled onto the wood chips on my butt. He stomped on my hand and kept his foot pressed down on top of my fingers. Then Lizzie slid out of the tunnel, stood up between us, and held her hand up to Craig's chest. As soon as she touched him, he flinched, as though he hadn't seen her. Which I guess was true. "Yow!" Craig said. "Where did you come from?"

"That's not important right now. Listen,"

Lizzie said, "I'm sorry we were eavesdropping on you, but you can't beat up Willie."

"Sure I can," Craig growled. "I could beat him up blindfolded, one-handed, hopping on one foot. Just watch me."

"Well, yeah," I said, figuring my only chance was to keep Craig talking. He might have been nice to his little brother, but he was killing my fingers. I tried not to think about what he could do to the rest of me. "Of course you could beat me up if I was blindfolded, one-handed, hopping on one foot. But where would the challenge be in that? In a fair fight, I'd probably kick your oversized, hairy—"

"Shut UP, Willie!" Lizzie and Craig both said at once. Then they looked at each other, rattled. Lizzie recovered first. I hoped she knew what she was doing—my hand was killing me. "As I was saying, you can't beat up Willie, because he and I are the only ones who can help you."

"What are you talking about? And make it fast, because you already made me miss my bus. I have to get going soon, or I'll have to rush while I'm pounding on Willie, and it will ruin the fun."

"Craig, we heard the part about your little brother. If you let us go, we can get the cell phone to him without your parents even knowing about it."

Flynn stared at her. "You're serious? You can really bring him the phone? And you would do that—for me? Then what would I have to do for *you* to make it even?"

"Yes, we could really do it. Yes, we would do it for you. And you wouldn't owe us anything."

"Well," I interjected, "you might consider getting off my hand." Craig lifted his foot, but reached down and grabbed the back of my collar in an iron death grip. I yanked my bruised fingers away, sat up, and started to put my newly burned sneaker back on.

"How are you planning on doing this?"

Lizzie said, "We can't tell you that. But I promise your brother will get the phone. Just tell us where he lives, and let us get going. Little Tyler won't have to wake up scared and alone tonight."

Craig said, "You promise? Really?" Lizzie nodded, and he handed her the phone. "Just tell him that you're friends with Craigie-weggie, all right? I taught him never to talk to strangers, but that way he'll know you're okay."

"Craigie-weggie?" I asked.

"Look, Willie, I could still totally kill you."

Lizzie said, "Come on, Willie, we don't have time for this. We have to go get the—um, we have to go get the object we need. Craig, just give us your ex-stepdad's address, okay?"

"It's Two Seventy-seven Swamp Court, in Frogtown, the trailer right near the edge of the water. You can't miss it, but watch out for Tyler's dad's pit bulls. I think there are three of them."

Lizzie said, "Got it—Two Seventy-seven Swamp, Frogtown, three pit bulls. Let's hit the road, Willie."

Craig said, "One more thing: Don't tell anyone about this, okay?"

"Your secret's safe with us, Craigie-weggie," I said, and took off running toward home. As I passed Craig, I saw Lizzie pat him on the shoulder. Then she was running beside me. Behind us, Craig shouted, "Hey, wait! How did you know my brother's name?" But we didn't even look back.

As we left, Lizzie confirmed my alarming suspicion: Her plan was to fly the magic carpet to Tyler's house. She told me to get Dodger while she "made some preflight arrangements." I asked her whether her arrangements would include finding out how to get to little Tyler's killer-dog-infested house. She said she'd find out how to get there, no problem. I said, "Magic?" She said, "Mapquest."

I limped home on my sore, enchanted toe, which rubbed against the ground through the gaping hole in my sneaker. Between that, my throbbing hand, and my black eye, I was starting to feel like I'd been through a war. And we still had a carpet flight to get through.

I had no problem persuading my parents to let me go back out. I think the Tincture of Distraction was still working, because my dad didn't even ask me how the big speech had gone. In fact, my parents didn't really pay much attention to me unless I was touching them. Amy was a different story. She kept staring at me, then looking away, then looking around again in bewilderment. I knew my problems with her were far from over.

I went upstairs, got Dodger, and headed out the back door into the woods. On the way over, I kind of thought he'd be mad at me for having switched the order of the assembly speeches, but all he did was slap me on the back and say, "Willie, that was a great plan! Dude, I never doubted you for a second!" I tried not to roll my eyes.

When we got to the Field of Dreams, I told Dodger about the mission to Craig's brother's house. He thought it was a great idea, but there was a catch: He couldn't go with us. Apparently, he couldn't help an Irish kid directly either. "But this will be great," he said. "My two best flying students of this century on a combat mission together!"

"What do you mean, best of this century? Aren't we your ONLY flying students of this century?"

"Well, yeah, technically. But, dude, I taught lots of people how to fly in other centuries."

"Like who?"

"Um, Amelia Earhart, the Red Baron, and . . . let's see . . . oh, I almost forgot: Captain Max Pruss." I looked at Dodger blankly. "You know," he said. "The pilot of the *Hindenburg* zeppelin."

"So, Dodger, your three best flight students of the whole twentieth century all crashed?"

"Uh, in a sense . . . I mean, if you're going to be all precise about it . . . hey, look! There's Lizzie!"

The next thing I knew, Dodger was saying, "Bon voyage, dudes! Beware of—"

The end of his sentence was drowned out by the rush of wind as Lizzie and I took off on the Flying Carpet of Khartoum. Lizzie asked, "Did he just say we should beware of cannibals?" I shrugged; I was pretty busy concentrating. I was mostly controlling the flight, with Lizzie standing next to me, holding a fistful of my sweatshirt with one hand and reading the directions aloud. Interestingly, we could see each other. Dodger had said that the Tincture of Distraction and the magic of the carpet would probably cancel each other out. I have to say, I did a lot better on this mission than I had on my first one. Lizzie kept telling me I should go faster, but hey, we were getting there. At one point, she dug her elbow into me and pointed out two little kids below us in a little red wagon. They appeared to be going faster than we were, but they were going downhill—so it was a totally unfair comparison.

Anyway, we eventually got to Frogtown and found the trailer at the edge of the swamp where

Tyler lived with his dad and the three deadly dogs. Once we didn't need the directions anymore, Lizzie whipped Tyler's cell phone out of her pocket, handed it to me, and said, "Okay, Willie, I'll take it from here."

"What do you mean, you'll take it from here?" I asked.

"Look, do you see those high-voltage power lines running on both sides of the trailer? And that row of trees in front? And the clotheslines in the back by the swamp? Ooh, and the agitated, snarling dogs?"

I gulped. "Uh, yeah. But I could—"

"I think we're going to have to come in at a pretty steep angle if we want to get to Tyler's window without getting fried, smashed, or eaten. So while I know you are more than capable of piloting this carpet, I just thought you might want to give me a turn, that's all."

I could feel the clammy sweat of intense physical fear breaking out all over my body. "Well," I said, "I guess it's only fair that I give you a chance."

"I knew you'd see it my way," Lizzie said. "Now hold on! I'm going to have to dive almost vertically to get us past the power lines with enough speed to outrun the dogs. Then we'll circle the trailer once to get the dogs confused. They shouldn't be able to see us, but they will smell us. We'll need to hover by Tyler's window for a moment while you lean over the side of the carpet, knock on the window, and give him the phone, and we'll want to have a head start. Any questions?"

"Uh, couldn't we just land on the roof of the trailer? Or knock on the door?"

"No, the roof isn't flat, see? And we can't knock on the door. Craig said his ex-stepdad would be mad about the phone thing if he knew about it, remember? So we need to get the phone to Tyler without his father knowing about it. Now hold on!"

I grabbed the hood of Lizzie's windbreaker, and she shifted her weight forward. There was a horrible moment when we were tilted forward but hadn't started to dive yet—kind of like that feeling when you're momentarily balanced at the top of a roller coaster. Then the wind was rushing past my face, the power lines were getting bigger and bigger right in front of me, and the dogs were starting to bark.

Wow, those were some loud dogs.

Not only that, but they appeared to be staring right at us. "Uh, Lizzie," I said.

"Hush," she said, "I'm trying to concentrate. You don't want me to hit any power lines, do you?"

"No, but I don't think Dodger said—"

"Not now, Willie! I have to—oops! Oh, dear!" Lizzie swerved to avoid a power pole, and the front edge of the carpet caught a tree branch. Instantly, we were tumbling and spinning at the same time. Lizzie was clutching my coat, I was desperately trying to grab the edge of the carpet, and the ground was getting really big, really fast.

The impact was brutal. We landed about fifty feet behind the trailer, only about a yard from the beginning of the mucky swamp. Lizzie was on top of me, and the carpet had ended up half-submerged amid the reeds, maybe ten feet away from us. Lizzie just had time to gasp, "Willie, are you all right?" before the dogs got to us.

All three of them stood in front of our prone bodies, growling and drooling. No doubt about it, they had totally watched us flying in. "Lizzie," I said, "I don't think Dodger told us to beware of cannibals. Looking back on it, I'm pretty sure he said *beware of animals*."

As the dogs glared at us right at our eye level, Lizzie muttered, "Oh, right. Good one, Willie."

For maybe ten seconds, we didn't move and neither did the dogs. Then they all started barking at once. Lizzie rolled off me, and I jumped up. I don't know what got into me, but I said, "I'll hold them off. Get the carpet!" Thinking fast, I tried to come up with something I could use as a weapon. There was absolutely nothing, but I figured I might be able to get the dogs away from Lizzie. As the dogs started jumping toward my face, I pulled off my left sneaker and threw it. "Fetch!" I shouted. All three dogs turned and rushed after the sneaker. The one that got there first pounced, and in an instant there were little shreds of leather and rubber flying everywhere. But then that dog started stumbling around in circles, looking totally confused. *Wow*, I realized, *the Tincture of Distraction works on the dogs! At least if they eat some* . . . Too bad there were still two more dogs, and I only had one more sneaker. I whipped that one off my right foot, tossed it as far as I could, and watched the two remaining dogs jump on it. Only one of them turned back toward me. Before I could come up with Plan B, the last dog was hurtling through the air at me. I fell on my back and tried to kick at him with my bare feet. My burned big toe brushed against the fur of his belly, and instantly, the dog twisted away from me. He sniffed at the air, but didn't look back in my direction. The tincture on my foot was still working! He couldn't see me! I was saved! This was great.

But he was still growling. And now he was looking over my right shoulder at something in the swamp. "Lizzie," I said in the calmest voice I could muster, "I think you might want to hurry with that carpet."

CHAPTER TWELVE

From the Office
of Doctor Chimpstone

LATER THAT NIGHT, back at the Field of
Dreams, we told Dodger about the whole adven-
ture: how Lizzie had half-run, half-swum her way
through the swamp, gotten the carpet just in time,
and swooped in to pick me up—just as Tyler's dad
had come outside to see what all the racket was.
How the dad had said, "All right, Killer! Down,
Slash! Relax, Muffy! If you give me a minute, I'll
take you for a nice walk. Stay here, Tyler." And how,
as soon as Daddy was gone, we had delivered the
cell phone, as promised. I think Dodger especially

liked the part where we'd told Tyler that Craigie-weggie had sent us.

"Dudes, that is awesome! No, that's better than just awesome—that's, like, *made* of awesome! It went just as I planned, too!"

Lizzie and I just rolled our eyes at each other and walked out of the woods toward home. In my backyard, I realized that I was shoeless, scratched up, and smeared all over with swampy muck. I didn't want my parents to see me in this state, so I tiptoed through the door, crept up the stairs, and eased my way along the wall to the bathroom. I turned the corner and reached for the light switch. A hand covered mine. I stifled a scream and flipped the switch. Amy was standing there, in her pj's, with her Sherlock hat firmly in place. "A-ha!" she said triumphantly.

You know, I'm not sure Amy totally bought my story about how Lizzie and I had been abducted by swamp-dwelling aliens from the planet Murgh. But she did get out of the bathroom without making a commotion, which allowed me to take a shower before my parents figured out I was home. Some days, that's the best a brother can hope for.

When Lizzie and I got off the school bus the next morning, Craig was waiting for us. He shook my hand so hard that I thought he might rip it off and actually hugged Lizzie. "Thank you," he whispered. "My brother had a horrible dream last night. When my phone rang, I was so relieved. I kept thinking, *What if he hadn't been able to call me? What if—*"

James Beeks interrupted our touching little scene. "Craig," he hissed, "what are you doing? You're *hugging* the enemy!"

"Just relax, James, okay? It's an election, not World War Three," Lizzie said.

"Shows how much you know," James snapped. "There hasn't even been a World War Three. Now, Craig, step away from this stupid, ugly—"

Suddenly Craig moved so fast that he was a blur. James fell to the ground, clutching his face. Then Craig was standing next to me, breathing hard and shaking his fingers through the air. "That *hurt*," he said.

James looked up and said, "You think it hurt *you*?" His hands fell to his sides, and I could see that the area around his right eye was already swelling massively where Craig had just punched it.

Then the teacher in charge of the bus lines came over, took one look at James, and sent all four of us to the office. This was terrible. After all we had done the night before to get Tyler's cell phone to his house, now Craig would get suspended and lose *his* cell phone. It was almost enough to make me wish James hadn't gotten punched in the eye.

Almost.

The secretaries stuck us in a little back room that connected to the principal's office, warned us to behave, and closed the door. I stared at Craig. Craig stared at Lizzie. Lizzie stared at James. James rubbed his eye. Then Lizzie said, "Hey, look! The initials *C.F.* are carved on my chair."

Without looking up, James said, "Duh. Craig's initials are carved on *every* chair in this room. Right, Craig?"

Craig said, "Look, James, I'm sorry I punched you. But why do you have to be so *mean* all the time?"

James didn't answer. Craig sighed and said, "Oh, man, I don't believe this! Now my mom's going to take away my cell phone for sure."

Lizzie said, "Maybe not. Hey, James, if Craig gets suspended, you won't have a running mate, right? And then you'll probably have to forfeit the election."

James snarled, "I'm not going to forfeit the election. I refuse! Black eye or not, I can still whup your geeky, weirdo bu—"

"So, as I was saying, it would be good for you if we found a way to let Craig off the hook."

"Let him off the hook? He *punched* me! Plus, why should you want him to get away with this? If he gets suspended, you win."

"Yes," Lizzie said. "But I'd rather win this thing fair and square. Also, Craig did something that really made me happy."

"What did he do that was so great?" James asked.

"He punched you," Lizzie said, smiling sweetly. "Now, the way I see it, we could say that Willie punched you . . ."

"No way!" James interjected.

". . . or maybe it would be better if we said that *I* punched you . . ."

"*Me* get punched by a girl? Who would believe *that*?"

Lizzie chuckled. "I know a lot of people who would have no trouble at all believing that."

"Well, I won't do it! No *way* will I say that either of you gave me this black eye."

Then Craig spoke up. "Guys, don't worry about it. I punched James, and I'll take the punishment. I mean, it's no big deal. I just realized something, anyway: I don't need my cell phone for Tyler to call me. As long as he has his cell phone, he can just call my house. It's not the end of the world. Besides, I never really wanted to be vice president anyway. I only agreed to run so James's parents wouldn't think he was a failu—"

"That's ENOUGH!" James said. "Fine, I'll just go in there and say I didn't see anything. The rest of you can say whatever the heck you want. Just be quiet about me and my parents, Craig. I mean it."

Craig nodded.

Then the principal's door opened. Her name is

Dr. Whistleblower. I had never been sent to her before, but I knew she was a scary lady. Mostly she just hid in her office, but I'd heard stories. Some kids said she had a pet cobra that she kept in the bottom drawer of her desk. Others said the candy on her little coffee table was made of truth serum, and that if you ate even one piece, you'd be willing to rat out your own mother. And this one second grader who hangs out with my sister swears that she once saw Dr. Whistleblower on a daytime TV talk show about people with violent personality disorders. According to this kid, Dr. W. was throwing chairs around the set, shouting, "You want a piece of me?" Watching Dr. W. now as she cracked her knuckles and gave us the evil eye, I had no trouble believing that last story.

I don't know how long it usually takes for a kid to crack in that office, but I'm proud to say that even after maybe twenty minutes of threats, bribe offers, and out-and-out blackmail, none of us told Dr. Whistleblower anything. She had just announced that if we didn't talk, she would have to suspend us all, when I heard *POOF,* and Dodger appeared behind her. He was holding his blue telephone in one hand and a spray bottle labeled ESSENCE OF BELIEF in the other.

Craig and James didn't react at all, of course, because they couldn't see Dodger. But Lizzie looked at me with panic in her eyes. Dodger smiled at us and mouthed, *Don't worry, dudes. I've got this under control!* Then he sprayed the air in front of Dr. Whistleblower's face. I put my head in my hands; I couldn't bear to see what happened next.

When Dr. W.'s phone rang a moment later, I must have jumped about three feet. She picked it up and said, "Hello, this is Dr. Whistleblower."

I looked up. Dodger's lips were moving, but I couldn't hear the words. Dr. W. sat up straighter in her chair, covered the mouthpiece of her phone, and said, "Ooh, it's the State Department of Education! They're calling about your case."

Dodger gave us the thumbs-up sign. I swear, I almost fainted.

"Yes, Dr. Chimpstone. I'm honored that you're calling me today. Yes, of course I'll put us on speakerphone."

Now Dodger's voice was coming through the

phone's speaker. He said, "Guess what, dude? I mean, lady dude."

Dr. W. looked puzzled but said, "What? Umm . . . state dude?"

"This is your lucky day! Here at the State Department of Education's Division of Complicated and Pointless Paperwork (Triplicate Filings Division), we've invented a new suspension form, and you've been selected as the very first principal in the entire state who gets to use it. And we understand you will get to fill it out FOUR times! This will be great. Unfortunately the computer version isn't quite ready yet, but that's all right. I hope you have a lot of pens handy."

Oh, come on, Dodger, I thought. *You sound like a half-surfer, half-school-boss. And a handwritten form? Dr. W. is an intelligent, professional educator. With or without a magic belief spray, there's no way she's going to buy your act.*

"I'm sure my secretary has plenty of pens she can use to fill out your new form, Dr. Chimpstone."

Okay, maybe she was buying it.

Dodger threw back his head and laughed. "Oh, that's a good one! I knew you were, like, a totally impressive law-and-order principal, but I didn't know you also had such an excellent sense of humor. I'm sure you're familiar with Regulation G-Nine, which clearly states that all suspension paperwork must be personally filled in by the principal herself, in triplicate. So that's, uh, thirteen forms you'll need to fill out for the four students in front of you."

"Actually, sir, four times three is twelve." Dr. W. said this with a bit of attitude, but I noticed she was looking a bit pale and shaky all of a sudden.

"Oh, right. Dude, no *wonder* they kicked me out of the Division of Multiplication. Just kidding. Get it, though? Division of Multiplication? See, because division and multiplication are opposites, so that's a totally funny name for a—well, anyway, you are correct. You'll only have to fill out the form twelve times, then. Whew! That will save you about nineteen pages of writing. Well, plus the D-Seventeen form: Permission to Staple Multiple Handwritten Copies."

"So," Dr. W. said, "you're telling me I have to fill out twelve copies of a nineteen-page form— personally? By *hand*?"

"Yes, Dr. Whistleblower, you are the chosen

one. We here at the state know that, while many other, less-determined principals might choose to let these four children go due to the total lack of evidence, you wouldn't let a measly seven hours of boring hand-copying get between you and the, uh, administration of justice. Right?" He gave a hearty chuckle.

Dr. W. made a weak attempt to laugh in response, but what came out of her sounded like the last cry of a strangled crow. Her skin was losing all of its color, too. "Uh, right. That's me: Dr. Justice!"

"Perfect!" Dodger shouted. "Then we'll fax you the instructions for filling out Form DP-Seven, as well. That's the Illustration of Incident Scene in Pastel Watercolors. Dude, this one is amazing! I invented it myself. All you have to do is paint a life-size six-panel series of illustrations, showing the progress of the incident. Per student, of course. I have to warn you, the instructions are a bit long. They were written by my brother, umm, Dr. Rodger Chimpstone. I hope you have a lot of paper in your fax machine!"

Dr. W. just sat there staring at the speaker in horror. I swear, her face was absolutely gray.

"Hello?" Dodger said. "Are you, like, still with me?"

Dr. W. cleared her throat. "Uh, yes, sir."

"Great! Then I think you should get started on that paperwork. If you tackle this right away, I don't see any reason why you shouldn't be able to leave your office by—oh, I don't know—next Friday afternoon? If you'd like, we can get you some food and water. I'll just send over a form X-Thirty-one: Application for Liver and Surplus Cheese on Dampened Onion Bread."

Dr. W. wiped her clammy-looking forehead and said, "Um, sir. On second thought, perhaps I will give these children a second chance. After all, what's justice without mercy, right?"

Dodger sighed. "Dr. Whistleblower, are you absolutely, like, sure about this? I know how much you enjoy suspending children, and I wouldn't want to do anything to spoil your fun. Plus, dude, the pastel painting part is, like, completely off the hook! I'm sure you'd have a great time with the—"

Dr. W. said, "You're right, Dr. Chimpstone. I do enjoy a nice suspension. But then again, we have to consider what's best for the children. So someone else will just have to try out your, um, wicked awesome new form."

"All right, if you insist. I won't take up any more of your time. Although, if you'd like to give these kids a firm scolding, I would be happy to send you Form FS-Ninety-seven: Scolding, Intimidation, and General Causation of Students' Nightmares, Condensed Version. It's only seventy-three pages long, and we'll gladly send along a magnifying glass to help you read the last nineteen pages of instructions. They're in Japanese, but I'm sure you could—"

"That won't be necessary, but thanks anyway. I'm sure this is all just a misunderstanding. Right, kids? Now, why don't you all just scamper back to class and we'll pretend this whole thing never happened?"

"All righty, then," Dodger said. "I'll just have my brother call you next week to see how things are going. Later!"

Dr. W. shooed us out of her office and hung up. Dodger smiled, put away his phone, sat down in the corner, and started munching on a banana. Dr. W. reached into her desk's bottom drawer and pulled out a gallon jug of Pepto-Bismol. I had a feeling she'd need to keep it handy for a while. As we walked away, I thought I heard her mutter: "A form for scolding? My goodness, the Department of Education takes the fun out of everything."

On the way upstairs, James said, "What the heck was up with *that*? The haunted playground, my speech getting all jumbled up, and now the principal lets us all *walk*? Does it seem to any of you like things have been getting a little weird around here?"

"No," I said, trying not to crack a smile.

"Uh-uh," said Lizzie.

"Nope," said Craig. "Just another busy day on the campaign trail."

At the top of the steps, James turned left, toward the nurse's office. Good move—he really needed to get some ice on that eye. The rest of us turned right and headed for Mrs. Starsky's room. Just before we went in, Craig said, "Hey, guys, you know we're still going to be enemies in the election, right?"

"Absolutely. But from here on in, what if we all agreed to just play fair?" Lizzie said.

Craig raised one eyebrow, then shrugged and said, "Why not? I'll try anything once!" And with that, we stepped into the room together.

CHAPTER THIRTEEN

The Shocking Truth About Recess

AFTER SCHOOL, I went to Lizzie's house to help her with her speech, which she would be giving the next morning. I felt kind of funny about being there. I mean, Lizzie had been to my house a bunch of times, and her parents had been driving me places for years. Plus, I'd been in her house for little bits of time before, but this was different. Now I was *hanging out at Lizzie's house*. Lizzie's mom offered us tea and biscuits, which sounded totally revolting—but it turns out that English people call cookies biscuits. We sat around the kitchen table and told Mrs. Barrett all about the events of the campaign so far, leaving out the parts with magic, flight, and/or packs of vicious dogs. She said, "Wow, this is so exciting! My little girl is conquering America!" Lizzie rolled her eyes. I knew the feeling.

When we finally tore ourselves away from the tea, cookies, and embarrassment, I found myself in Lizzie's room. I was *hanging out in Lizzie's room*! Apparently, so was Dodger, who appeared out of thin air the instant we sat down. Thankfully, there were two chairs, so I didn't have to sit on a girl's bed. Besides, Dodger immediately took to jumping up and down on it.

"All right, Elizabeth," I said formally. "I have devoted some serious thought to this last speech, and I feel that the time has come to discuss the issues with the voters. The way I see it, the people want to know where we stand on such serious matters as the improvement of the school salad bar, procedures for decreasing wasted recess time, and developing a mechanism for taking student complaints to the PTA."

Lizzie said, "And what do we plan to do about those issues?"

"I have no idea," I replied. "But hey, I'm not the one who tricked me into running for president."

Dodger stopped doing back handsprings on Lizzie's bed long enough to say, "Dudes, don't sweat the small stuff. People don't care about the issues—they want to vote for someone they like. So you're golden. Willie is the cool-walking, smooth-talking bringer of doughnuts. And James is the guy who can't even give a speech without offending half the audience. Plus he got totally hooked in the eye by his own running mate. All Lizzie has to do is remind everyone why you're the true-blue choice, and the next thing you know, you'll be wearing the crown!"

"Uh, Dodger," I said, "I know what you mean, but . . . well . . . James isn't the only one with a black eye. And what about all the people who laughed at me because of James's posters? They don't think I'm so cool. Oh, and another thing: Presidents don't even wear crowns."

"Sure they do. Whenever I see Miss America on TV, she always has a crown. Which reminds me—when's the swimsuit competition? I think we should get you into a weight-lifting program to bulk up your chest muscles before—"

"Dodger! The Miss America pageant and the presidency are two totally different things! They have absolutely NOTHING to do with each other."

"No way! *Oh, man!* That means I made Abe Lincoln parade around in swim trunks and a sash for nothing, huh? No wonder Mrs. L. never invited me back to their big white house after the election."

"Wait a minute!" Lizzie exclaimed. "Dodger is absolutely right!"

I was stunned. "You mean, there really is a swimsuit competition? Because I am *not* gonna—"

"No, you fool, he's right about the election! All I need to do is remind everyone of how great you are!"

"Oh, so I'm a *great* fool?"

"Yes," she said happily. "You really are! Now, go home. You, too, Dodger. I have work to do!"

Lizzie refused to let me see her speech before the assembly, so I was pretty nervous as the big event got started. Just like the last time, she and

I were sitting on one side of the stage, and Craig and James were on the other. My black eye had faded to a pale, sickly yellow, but James's was in full, gruesome effect. I kind of felt sorry for him, at least until Craig stepped up to the microphone:

Dear classmates, fellow students, teachers, and staff,

I was really not sure what I should say today. I mean, on the one hand, you all know that this is my second time in fifth grade. So maybe I'm not that smart. Or maybe I'd make an extra-good vice president, since I have more years of elementary-school experience than just about anybody. But the main thing that confuses me is what I should tell you about James and Willie.

I mean, I made an agreement with Willie and Lizzie yesterday that we wouldn't pull any dirty tricks today—we all agreed that the election should be fair and square. So does that mean I shouldn't point out that Willie's nickname has always been "Wimpy"? I mean, I don't want to be unfair. And does it mean I shouldn't point out that, even though Willie's posters showed him in a baseball uniform like he's a big ball hero, really he only got one hit all season?

I mean, I don't want to be unfair. So maybe I shouldn't even mention that Willie hasn't ever been involved with student government before, or that Lizzie has only been in this country since the third grade, even though in the real grown-up elections, you can't run for president unless you were born in America.

Because, you know, I don't want to be unfair.

[NOTE: I was getting pretty annoyed at this point. Either Craig was really, really innocent, or he was a political genius. Unless Beeks had actually written the speech.]

So instead of pointing out the many problems with Willie and Lizzie, I've decided to focus on why you should vote for my good friend, Mr. James Beeks. James is a leader. James is the guy who had the most hits of any player in the history of fall Little League. He's also the best quarterback in the town football league, and captain of the wrestling team.

James Beeks is clutch. James Beeks comes through. He's the kind of guy you want to follow. As you know, James has also been involved in student government longer

153

than anybody else. And he has really made some great changes in our school.

For example, do you remember the Great Recess Ball Controversy of 2008? I wonder how many of you know that it was James Beeks who came up with the famous A to Z Compromise. For all of you kindergarteners, I'll explain what happened. Last year, the big kids were having massive battles every day over which class should get first pick of the balls for recess. There were arguments in the hallways, near-riots in the lunchroom. For a while, it was student against student, teacher against teacher. Until James Beeks came up with his idea: that for the first half of the rest of the year, classes would pick balls in alphabetical order based on the first letter of their teacher's last name.

And then, to make things fair, for the rest of the year, classes would pick balls in _reverse_ alphabetical order based on the _last_ letter of their teacher's last name.

Needless to say, James's great compromise went through. And there was joy in the halls, peace on the playground, a better school for all of us.

Because that's what James Beeks is really about: a better school for you and me.

Thank you.

[NOTE: Oh, barf. That speech was so corny you could put it in the microwave and pop it. I hoped Lizzie's speech wasn't like that.]

The whole room burst into applause, and Craig stood there for a moment, taking it all in. After all, it's not like Craig had experienced many victories in his academic career. But then, gradually, a strange hush came over the crowd, as everybody realized that one girl was standing up right in the middle of the first row. I couldn't believe this: It was Amy. She was raising her hand. Craig had no idea what to do. I'm sure Mrs. Starsky had no idea what to do either. And before she could figure it out, Amy spoke.

Her high-pitched second-grader voice carried to every corner of the room. "Excuse me, Mr. Flynn? I have a question." The whole roomful of people stared as Amy took a deep breath and continued, "You know how James came up with that whole compromise thing?"

Craig nodded.

"Well, wasn't James's teacher that year named Mrs. Alabaz?"

Craig nodded again, wondering where she was going with this. I was wondering the same thing.

"So then, for the first half of the rest of the year, his class got to pick a ball first, right? Because her name starts with *A*."

Craig said, "Uh, I guess that's true."

"And then, for the second half of the year, when it went in reverse order, by the last letter of the teacher's name, James's class still got to pick first, because the last letter of her name was a *Z*. Isn't that true?"

Craig had to think about it for a bit, but then he nodded.

"So really, James's so-called compromise simply made sure his own class would always be first."

Craig stared at her, openmouthed. So did everybody else.

"I'm just sayin'," Amy concluded, and sat down. In the long, awkward silence that followed, Craig kind of crept his way back to his seat; I could see his whole face was red. Then Mrs. Starsky recovered, and introduced Lizzie. I sweated my way through her speech, which went like this:

Hello, everyone. I have to admit, Craig was right about several important facts. For one thing, he is absolutely right that James Beeks is a natural leader. If you give him the chance, he will lead, and you will follow. In fact, you'll be glad to follow, and you will feel great about doing what James Beeks says, and thinking what James Beeks tells you to think. Unfortunately I don't think you really want to go where James Beeks wants you to go.

As an example—and Craig was right about this, too—I was not born in America. I came here from England in the middle of third grade. I remember that day so well. I was so excited to be in this beautiful new country, to make amazing new friends. I even put on my best, fanciest red winter jacket because I wanted to make a great first impression. Then, when I got introduced to my class, James Beeks started shouting, "She's a redcoat! She's a redcoat!" And the entire class followed—because James Beeks is a leader. In fact, there were only two kids in the whole room who didn't join in the cruel chant. One of them was my running mate, Willie Ryan. James led the class, but Willie did the right thing. Which kind of president do you want?

Now I'd like to say a few words about my best friend, Willie Ryan. Oh, some of you might laugh, but it's true: Willie is my best friend, and I'm proud of it. I have to admit he doesn't look like much—

[NOTE: Thanks for pointing that out to the whole school, Lizzie.]

—but if you knew Willie like I do, you'd see him for the great candidate he really is. I've seen Willie fight a raging fire. I've seen Willie sweat and bleed to get better at baseball so that he wouldn't let his team down in their big last game of the season. So he might have only had the one big game, but that wasn't luck. That was the hard work and courage of Willie Ryan.

But this election shouldn't be about sports. There is no doubt that James is a better athlete than Willie—but tomorrow when you step into that voting booth, you won't be electing a quarterback. You'll be electing a president. And no matter how much James tries to convince you otherwise, that isn't the same thing.

I have more examples of the goodness of Willie Ryan.

How about the time Willie stepped in between me and three angry pit bulls? How many of you would have done the same thing for your best friends? How many of you have faced an angry Craig Flynn? I have to tell you: Willie has.

So you can vote for James Beeks if you want a quarterback or if you are looking for chances to get led around into doing things you won't be proud of. But if you want a good, honest, kind, brave, smart president—someone you can trust to take care of your best interests—please vote for Willie Ryan, the true-blue candidate.

Lizzie looked at me and held out her hand in my direction. I couldn't believe it: People clapped. They actually CLAPPED for me, Willie Ryan! It was astounding. When Lizzie came back to sit next to me, I whispered, "Did you really mean all that stuff?"

"What stuff?"

"Like, do you really think I'm good, honest, kind, and brave?"

"Absolutely."

"Am I really your best friend?"

"Duh."

"And do you really think I'm smart?"

"Well, Will, in order to get elected, sometimes a politician has to, um, bend the truth a little bit. . . ."

"Oh, be quiet," I said.

All in all, it was a pretty good assembly.

At the bus stop after school, Amy stopped me and Lizzie. I started to thank Amy for the brilliant question she had asked Craig during the assembly, but she shrugged that off. As soon as the bus pulled away and left us alone at the corner, Amy turned to both of us and said, "Okay, I've helped you with this election all along. Now I'm fairly sure I've figured out the secret of your campaign. I promise I won't tell anybody, but I just want to know if I'm right. Is that fair?"

I shrugged. Lizzie pushed around some pebbles with the toe of her shoe.

"I said, is that fair?"

"Uh, I guess so," I mumbled.

Amy said, "Okay, so the way I see it, you're getting secret assistance from somebody large who has a low-pitched voice. We'll call him He Who Must Not Be Named. I notice that you're spending a lot of time in the woods. Also, our bananas have been disappearing at an alarming rate, and I've been finding blue hairs everywhere. My conclusion is this: Your secret campaign helper is an invisible blue orangutan!"

Lizzie and I stared at each other. I mean, what do you really say to that? Then we both burst out laughing.

"What's so funny?" Amy asked indignantly.

"An invisible blue orangutan!" I said. "Come on, Amy! Who ever heard of an invisible blue orangutan?"

"So you're denying the existence of this—this mystery primate?"

I turned to Amy, put on my straightest, most serious big brother face, and said, "I swear that I am not receiving secret campaign advice from an invisible blue orangutan. There! Are you satisfied?"

She gave me her toughest little-sister-detective look and said, "I believe you. But this investigation isn't over!" Then she stormed up the front walkway of our house. Lizzie turned to me and said, "Wow, Willie. That was an excellent, technically correct answer! Where did you learn to be so slick?"

"Well, Liz, in order to get elected, sometimes a politician has to, um, bend the truth a little bit. . . ." And then, right there on my front lawn, we broke out laughing again.

CHAPTER FOURTEEN

Election Day

THROUGHOUT THE NEXT DAY, classes got called down one by one. The teachers explained the voting system, and one by one, the kids went into the booth to pull a lever. If they pulled it to the right, James and Craig racked up a vote. If they pulled it to the left, Lizzie and I got the nod. Our class was the last to vote.

Mrs. Starsky called the four candidates aside and told us we'd be voting last of all. While the whole rest of the group lined up in front of us, and the line crawled forward, Craig said to Lizzie, "Good luck. And thanks for, uh, you know."

Lizzie said, "Good luck to you, too."

James turned to me and said, "May the best man win, Willie."

"And woman," Lizzie added.

"Maybe," said James, with a smirk.

My turn came. Mrs. Starsky patted my shoulder, smiled at me, and said, "Top of the pyramid, William!" I smiled back and entered the booth.

Snack Time

WHEN LIZZIE AND I got off the bus that day, we were alone. My mom had picked Amy up early for an orthodontist appointment. We still didn't know the results of the election, and I was kind of too nervous to go home by myself and sit there sweating it out. I invited Lizzie over, and she said yes.

My dad was downstairs in his office writing, so we didn't disturb him. We just went right upstairs, but I heard something coming from my room that stopped me cold. It was Dodger, singing:

Drop for drop
And day for day,
What you owe me
You will pay.

Ounce for ounce
And pound for pound,
Payback time
Will come around—

Oh yeah, doo be bop bop doooooo . . .

Lizzie and I exchanged worried glances, and knocked on my door. "Hey, buds!" Dodger said, waving a cracker at us. "Come on in! I was just having some mashed bananas with peanut butter, jelly, and tuna. It's really quite delicious. Hey, did you have a good election thing? Were you right about the whole lack-of-swimsuits issue? Because, Willie, if you want, you can borrow my spare surf shorts. I mean, I lend them to my brother all the time. I know they'd be a little on the large side, but they have a drawstring and—"

"Dodger," I said, "what was that song you were singing?"

"Why, do you like it? I'm proud to say I wrote the tune myself. And the *doo-be-bop-bop* part at the end. Pretty catchy, no? We chimpanzees are revered throughout the rain forest for our majestic songs of—"

"Dodger! Where did you get the words?"

"Oh, those? They're just a little spell that my old friend Lasorda cast on m—I mean, a little ditty that the Great Lasorda wrote. Why do you ask? It works, right? *Pound* does rhyme with *around,* doesn't it?"

Lizzie stomped her foot. "Dodger," she said, "Lasorda gave you the potion so you could go to school disguised as Willie, right?"

"Um, yeah, but—"

"Was that your idea, or his?"

"His, I guess."

"And then he gave you the Tincture of Distraction, right?"

"Yeah, but—"

"And the Essence of Belief?"

"Yeah, but—"

"So now you owe the Great Lasorda a really big favor?"

"Uh, not exactly."

"What do you mean, not exactly?" I asked.

"Three," Dodger said. "Actually, I owe him three favors. But it was totally worth it to help Willie get popular. I mean, Lasorda was just giving me a hand with Willie's Life Improvement Plan—for old times' sake. You don't think that's a problem, do you? I mean, he's a good friend of ours, right? So what could possibly go wrong?"

Lizzie and I sat down on both sides of Dodger. She put her left arm around him, and I did the same with my right. "Nothing," Lizzie said brightly. "Nothing at all."

In the silence that followed, Dodger reached under my bed and pulled out a smushed box. He held it out to us. "Cracker, dudes? You know, for dipping?"

"Dodger," I said, "I thought you'd never ask."

Go Fish!

GOFISH

JORDAN SONNENBLICK

What did you want to be when you grew up?
I wanted to be some combination of writer, teacher, and drummer. I never really thought I'd end up doing all three, though.

When did you realize you wanted to be a writer?
I don't remember exactly, but it was really, really early in life. However, I spent the first thirty-three years of my life bragging about how I was going to write a book someday, instead of actually working on my writing!

What's your first childhood memory?
Some kid named Anthony from down the block threw sand in my eyes, and my Grampa Sol sang the Sandman song to me until I calmed down and fell asleep. I just remember feeling so completely safe once I was all snuggled up with Grampa.

What's your most embarrassing childhood memory?
My eyes are terrible without my glasses on. Once at sleepaway camp when I was thirteen, I was showing off while waterskiing. In the middle of doing tricks on one ski, I crashed into a fifteen-foot-long wooden float. Afterward, I couldn't walk right for days!

What's your favorite childhood memory?
Watching the 1977 and 1978 World Series with my dad (The Yankees beat the Dodgers twice in a row!). Or when my parents got me my first drum set.

As a young person, who did you look up to most?
My Grampa Sol. He was a teacher and author, which drove me to pursue those careers as well. Also, he was the one person who never, ever lied to me. In my experience, kids appreciate honesty above nearly any other character trait.

What was your worst subject in school?
Sitting still. Come to think of it, that's still my worst subject.

What was your best subject in school?
Either English, or making my friends laugh. I haven't changed much, apparently.

What was your first job?
All through high school, I was both a tutor and a summer camp counselor. If you ever need help with algebra or archery, I'm your guy.

How did you celebrate publishing your first book?
With a big party in my backyard—a tent, catering, and even a Wiffle Ball game. Then my original publisher went out of business three days later. Yikes!

Where do you write your books?
Mostly at the computer in my kitchen, but sometimes on a laptop wherever I happen to be. As long as I have headphones with me, I'm pretty good at shutting out the world in order to write.

Where do you find inspiration for your writing?
From kids. My book ideas always start with a kid doing something that puzzles or amazes me. The Dodger books, for example, are inspired by events in my son's real life. No, he doesn't have a blue chimp for a best friend, but he does have many of the same worries and challenges Willie does.

Which of your characters is most like you?
Oh, gosh, ALL of them. No one character is 100% me, but each has big chunks of my personality, habits, strengths, and weaknesses. People who know me really well always say they can hear my voice in the words of each of my main characters.

When you finish a book, who reads it first?
My wife. In fact, she reads my pages daily while I'm writing every first draft. She's also the only person in the world whose judgment I never, ever ignore—which makes both my writing and my marriage better!

Are you a morning person or a night owl?
Both; I just need a nap in the middle of the day. I always tell my wife I should move to Spain so everyone around me would be taking a daily siesta, too.

What's your idea of the best meal ever?
My last Thanksgiving with my dad. I wish we could have had a hundred more just like it.

Which do you like better: cats or dogs?
Neither—I'm completely allergic! Well, that's not quite fair. I like dogs a lot, even if I don't like the itchy welts I get if I play with one for more than three minutes.

What do you value most in your friends?
Loyalty.

Where do you go for peace and quiet?
Any place where I can play an instrument or read. I also really like riding my bicycle out in the country where there's no traffic. In fact, whenever I get stuck in the middle of my writing, I find that a long bike ride is a great way to clear the jam and get my brain working again.

What makes you laugh out loud?
Just about anything. I laugh a lot.

What's your favorite song?
Just about anything the Beatles ever wrote. In fact, I love the Beatles so much that when each of my children was born, I made sure the Beatles album *Abbey Road* was the first music they heard.

Who is your favorite fictional character?
Probably Hagrid, from Harry Potter. He has such loyalty, and such a huge, brave heart.

What are you most afraid of?
Failing to come through for the people I love.

What time of year do you like best?
Baseball season. I spend the whole winter looking forward to the spring, when I can start pitching batting practice to my son and his friends again. Incidentally, I throw a pretty good two-seam fastball, a decent curve, and a killer cut fastball.

What's your favorite TV show?
I don't really have one. I guess my default answer would be any televised Yankees game.

If you were stranded on a desert island, who would you want for company?
My family. Or anyone who was good at shipbuilding.

If you could travel in time, where would you go?
Back to my old summer camp in the Poconos, around 1985. Or to the moment when either of my kids was born—there's just nothing else like becoming a parent.

What's the best advice you have ever received about writing?
If you want to get better at writing, you'd better read a lot. Most other writing advice is basically a matter of taste or opinion, but the connection between reading and good writing is a 100% non-negotiable fact. If I could, I'd carve this piece of advice above the doorway of every school in America.

What do you want readers to remember about your books?
I don't really think about what I'd like them to remember, but I hope that while they're reading, they come to care about my characters as much as I do.

What would you do if you ever stopped writing?
Go back to teaching. I really miss my old students. The great thing about working with middle schoolers is that no two days are ever the same, and I miss having that kind of fun randomness in my daily life.

What do you like best about yourself?
My thick, lustrous hair. Just kidding! Really, I am proud that I am kind, and that I try my best to make other people's lives easier. But I do, in fact, have thick and lustrous hair.

What is your worst habit?
Self-criticism.

What is your best habit?
I dunno, probably my addiction to reading.

What do you consider to be your greatest accomplishment?
Fatherhood.

Where in the world do you feel most at home?
At home. Or in NYC, Houston, Philly, or London. It's funny: I like big cities a lot—but being in my quiet little house with my family is better.

What do you wish you could do better?
Play guitar. I'm an okay player, but I am terrible about practicing.

What would your readers be most surprised to learn about you?
Maybe that I love to cook, but hate using recipes?

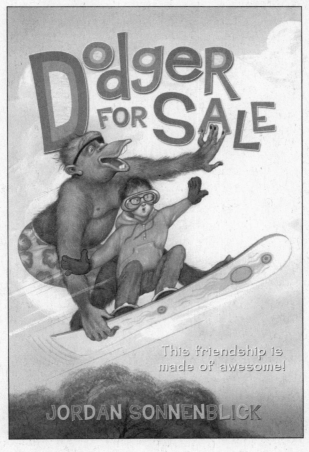

CHAPTER ONE

Whoopsie!

I'M STANDING AT THE TOP of a cliff. Well, according to the hand-lettered sign at the edge, it's technically a ski slope. But it looks pretty darn cliff-like to me. I have a snowboard attached to my feet, about a hundred pounds of hot, sweaty clothing on my body, and a pair of goggles strapped on over my glasses so I can't really see where the heck I'm going.

And there's a hyperactive blue chimp standing next to me. Despite the cold, he's sporting nothing but a pair of bright orange surf shorts and a black eye patch. And he's pretty excited. "Dude," he exclaims, "you OWN this slope! This is going to be so great!

Just remember, you've gotta BE the board. That's all you need to know—just BE the board. Oh, and don't fall and die. Because that would, like, totally ruin the plan."

I smile weakly at him. "The plan?" I ask.

"You know, bud. The *plan*. Step One: Totally carve up the top part of this slope. Step Two: Conquer the giant slalom course in the middle of the slope. Step Three . . . um . . . I told you about Step Three, right?"

"Is that the part where I get carried away on a stretcher?"

"No, Willie, that's Step Four. Just kiddin'! Actually, Step Three is the ski jump."

"SKI JUMP??? Dodger, you never told me there would be a ski jump! Are you crazy? I've never even tried snowboarding before, and now you expect me to go off of some gigantic ramp?"

"Dude, calm down. It's no biggie, okay? Everything's taken care of. See, we, um, fixed your board."

"What do you mean, you *fixed* my board? And who's 'we'?"

"The board is just a regular, ordinary snowboard, except the bottom has been painted with some—well, some special stuff. And never mind the 'we' thing."

"Special stuff? What kind of special stuff?"

Dodger gave me one of his patented one-eyed winks and said, "I came up with the formula myself . . . mostly. It's the same stuff that's on the bottom of the Magic Carpet of Khartoum. It should give you a little extra lift. At least, I'm pretty sure."

Oh, boy. The Magic Carpet of Khartoum is an actual, real-life flying carpet. And it's not very easy to control—trust me. So I can only imagine the kind of massive damage I can do when I try to combine flying with snowboarding. "Dodger," I say, "this is insane! Can you tell me again why I'm doing it?"

Dodger puts his hands on his hips and glares at me in exasperation. "Dude, do you want to save your little sister from the leprechauns or don't you?"

My life gets really complicated sometimes. This is one of those times. "Of course I want to save Amy! I just don't understand why we can't walk over to their field and ask them to give her back."

"Because that's exactly what they'll be expecting! Duh, do I have to think of everything around here?"

"Okay, I can see why we have to take the lepre-chauns by surprise. But why do I need to do the slalom course and everything?"

"'Cause, dude, it's cool! You never need a *reason* to be cool! Now, let's go over this one more time: Do you have your goggles?"

"Um, yeah. You're looking at me wearing them, aren't you?"

"Dude, you're just supposed to say, 'Check!'"

"Why?"

"'Cause it sounds awesome! Now, let's try again—we're running out of time! Goggles?"

"Check."

"Gloves?"

"Check."

"Map?"

"What map?"

"Oh, oops. Well, never mind that now. Alrighty, then—we'd better get moving! Any last questions?"

"Yeah! Where's Lizzie?" Lizzie is my best friend. And back then, she was also the only other person I knew who could see Dodger. He was totally invis-ible to everyone else.

Long story.

"Don't worry. She'll be there when it all goes down."

"When *what* all goes down?"

Just then something started beeping really, really loudly. I looked around, but the noise seemed to be coming from the side of Dodger's shorts. He reached into his pocket and pulled out something that looked like a cross between a cell phone, a GPS device, and a banana. Sure enough, it was the source of the beeps. It was also blinking bright orange once every few seconds. "Holy cow!" Dodger said. "Team Alpha is already in position! We've got to boogie!"

"We?"

"Yeah, we! You didn't think I was going to let you have all this fun by yourself, did you?"

"But . . . but . . . you don't have a snowboard!"

"Whoopsie. I knew I was forgetting *something*."

"Wait, so what are we going to do now?"

Dodger took maybe ten steps backward up the hill and said, "We are going to *fly*!" Then he charged toward me, leaped in the air, and landed on the board so his feet were right next to mine and his arms were around my waist. We started zooming down the hill.

That was when it occurred to me that I wasn't wearing a helmet.

"Cowabunga!" Dodger shouted in my ear. Then he laughed.

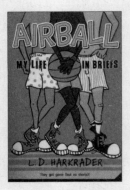